Praise for the writing of Z. A. Maxfield's *St. Nacho's*

"I found this story of love, hope, and redemption absolutely stunning and enthusiastically endorse it as a Recommended Read. *St Nacho's* is without a doubt one of the better books I have read in quite a while."

— Whitney, *Fallen Angel Reviews*

"Z.A. Maxfield is a truly brilliant author. *St. Nacho's* was an inspirational novel that will stay with you for a long time to come."

— Kimberley Spinney, *eCataromance*

"*St. Nacho's* is by far one of the most entrancing and emotional romances I've read in a long time and Z.A. Maxfield has certainly cemented her place in the keeper shelf of all m/m fans that like their characters with depth of emotion along with bone-melting sex!"

— Sabella, *Joyfully Reviewed*

"*St. Nacho's* is one of those stories where you're waiting for the other shoe to drop the whole time. It's an angst filled, edgy, story with a deep romance. I didn't want the story to end."

— Nikki, *Rainbow Reviews*

LooseId®

ISBN 10: 1-59632-883-5
ISBN 13: 978-1-59632-883-9
ST. NACHO'S
Copyright © April 2009 by Z. A. Maxfield
Originally released in e-book format in December 2008

Cover Art by Anne Cain
Cover Design by April Martinez

DISCLAIMER: Many of the acts described in our BDSM/fetish titles can be dangerous. Please do not try any new sexual practice, whether it be fire, rope, or whip play, without the guidance of an experienced practitioner. Neither Loose Id nor its authors will be responsible for any loss, harm, injury or death resulting from use of the information contained in any of its titles.

This book is an original publication of Loose Id. Each individual story herein was previously published in e-book format only by Loose Id and is a work of fiction. Any similarity to actual persons, events or existing locations is entirely coincidental.

Printed in the U.S.A. by
Lightning Source, Inc.
1246 Heil Quaker Blvd
La Vergne TN 37086
www.lightningsource.com

ST. NACHO'S

Z. A. Maxfield

Dedication

This one's for my Mom and Dad. Adopted kids are a grab bag of someone else's DNA; I don't think I realized how much until my little apples fell right off under the tree. Thanks for expecting the good, putting up with the bad, and loving me anyway!

Chapter One

I didn't plan, when I originally stopped, to stay for any length of time in Santo Ignacio. The tiny seaside town seemed a decent enough place to pull off the road and rest, so I rolled out my quilt on the sand next to the wall that butted up against the boardwalk and took a nap.

That no one rousted me, asked me what I was doing there, or gave me shit about transient this, homeless that, or vagrant whatever was the first clue I had that I might want to spend more than a somnolent hour there. When I rose it was dusk, and I had to pee so badly I took a chance and entered Nacho's Bar on the boardwalk. It was a sleepy little dive with a kind of cantina vibe where men were already lounging on the patio in the balmy ocean breeze sipping Coronas. They kicked back in beach clothes, licking salt off bronzed hands and biting into limes before knocking back shots of Cuervo.

These were *my* people.

That I was no longer one of them briefly irritated me as I asked the bartender if I could use the bathroom. He jerked his head as if to say, "Go ahead," even as he looked at me with a practiced eye. I probably presented an odd picture, dressed as I was in old jeans and an older motorcycle jacket with a club name emblazoned on the back. That had been a gift from a man who would no longer speak to me because I stole from him. I wouldn't be welcome in that club anymore, and I couldn't be too optimistic about my chances of being welcomed here.

The man stared at me, considering my piercings and the tat on my neck. I'd ridden hard all day and looked it, and I carried a battered violin case. Any one of those things made me appear odd in this place where everyone seemed healthy and laid-back, wearing fewer clothes than I, and I unconsciously tucked the instrument under my arm to make it less visible. *As if.*

I looked like the bike rode me here.

I went and used the bathroom, trying to get the worst of the dirt off my face and hands. It was actually an unexpected kindness, being allowed to use a bathroom in a bar when I hadn't purchased anything. I carefully tidied up the sink before I left. I went to the bar and asked if I could get a cup of coffee. The bartender served me one in a white ceramic coffee cup with a saucer, like at a diner, giving me little plastic creamer pods and a couple of sugar packets.

"Passing through?" he asked, and I was transported to a thousand different bars, most of which I only half-remembered, but all the same.

"Yeah," I said, setting my case down next to the stool. I was pulling my jacket off, making myself comfortable. I knew how to bar. "Nice here. I needed a rest."

"This is a good place for it," he said. He stared at me hard. "Notice anything unusual?"

"Nope," I said, stirring my coffee. "Should I?"

The bartender looked amused. He leaned over, elbows on the bar in a way I found provocative. He probably meant to shock me. "There aren't many women here right now," he said, waiting. "At all."

"What's your point?" I asked, knowing what it was. Really, I wasn't that into labeling myself, nor did I really want to share. I could see where he was headed, and I thought he probably wanted to shock the biker boy, but I just didn't have it in me at that moment.

"This is a gay bar, dude," he said, his eyebrows disappearing into the fringe on his forehead. *Fringe.* I got that from Neville, the Oxford bad boy who broke my nose the first time it was broken, after I'd been kicked out of Juilliard, but before I went home to my parents in disgrace. For an entire year, which would have been memorable if only I'd been sober enough to remember it, I'd lived in New York. There I sampled a sordid assortment of what I thought were sophisticated pleasures, including a month as the darling of the trust-fund set, followed by a fascination with BDSM clubs, a brief time as the pet of a motorcycle gang, and homelessness. It wasn't likely that anyone in this place could shock me.

"*Dude,*" I said, and I'm sorry to say I sort of mocked him, even though he'd been nothing but kind. I was tired. Shit happens. I looked around at the mellow crowd. "I could suck any one of these guys through fifty feet of irrigation pipe, but as it happens, today I'm not looking for love."

He tipped his head back and laughed, and I could see a smart-looking hickey under his jaw on the right. "Coffee's two bucks, refills on the house," he replied. He left to help some other patrons, but I felt a shift in the force of the room, as though, having made him laugh, the tension eased and life could return to normal. I shoved the rest of my creamer and sugar into my pocket and, taking my coffee with me, made for a corner of the patio where I figured I could smoke, and tried to remember if I knew what normal was.

The patio was enclosed by tall Plexiglas walls and heated by those large propane outdoor furnaces. It was so pleasant out there that I had an intense emotional moment of the kind that come over me now and then when I least expect it, and I turned my head away from the other patrons to hide it. I lit my cigarette with a shaking Zippo lighter I'd nicked off some guy in San Diego last month and figured that was another damn thing I had to make amends for. Shit. List was already a thousand fucking miles long and I couldn't go two days without adding to it.

I remembered I picked up his lighter when we went out behind the tiny restaurant to get busy. It was on the table and I thought I'd want to smoke after, to shut my mouth over the things I wouldn't want to say. When it was over, he tied the condom off and threw it in my face, and I sort of reacted to that with a little more force than strictly necessary. I had to get the hell out of Dodge before the manager came out and called the cops on us both.

Gotta love romance. I don't mind taking it up the ass against an alley wall, but nobody needs to disrespect me.

I angled my chair so I could smoke, drink my coffee, and pretend I was alone on the beach except for the occasional person strolling on the boardwalk. I don't know how long I sat there. It was full dark before I realized it, and the ashtray

I'd snagged was half full when the most beautiful hand I'd ever seen brought a coffeepot to hover over my cup, the long, elegant, and beautifully tapered fingers accented by a number of silver rings. I stared, fascinated by the relaxed and easy grip of that large hand, until I realized its owner was probably waiting to see if I wanted a refill. I looked up into a young man's face that was dazzling in its vitality. I nodded jerkily, recalling myself to the moment, and lowering my eyes under frank golden brown ones I would describe later as invasive, I watched that lovely boy fill my cup. For a moment, I almost saw the world in color. *Almost.*

At about ten o'clock I'd had as much coffee as a man could drink and also a plate of really first-rate nachos, for which the bar was famous, so I stopped by the bar to drop off my cup as a gesture of goodwill and asked if there was somewhere cheap in Santo Ignacio I could stay for the night. I did have some cash, not a lot, but I'd been longing for a bed and a shower for three days.

"If you don't mind the noise," said the bartender, "there's a studio upstairs. I used to live there when I first bought the place, but I moved in with my partner, and now I use it for storage more than anything. There's nothing up there but a bed and a bathroom and some file boxes." He considered me carefully. "You look like trouble slowing down."

I lowered my eyes again. It seemed I'd become the submissive's submissive. I didn't know what the hell I was besides three days tired and dirty. "I'd appreciate that for tonight. I could pay, work, or shag it off." No harm in being up front. He leaned over the bar again and put his head on his hand, resting it there.

"You've got nothing I need," he said, almost on a sigh. "Just trying to help." He held out a hand. "Jim."

"Thanks." I took it and gave it a manly shake. "Cooper. Sorry if I didn't sound…"

"It's all right, Cooper. Pleased to meet you. Don't try to come down here and drink after closing. The place has an alarm and cameras."

"I don't drink," I said. I don't…period. Never would again. He looked at me with eyes that said he'd heard it all. Not from me. *I don't drink*. I'd fucking kill myself first.

I picked up my violin and headed to my bike for my duffel. When I came back I mounted the stairs Jim had pointed out. They were in the corner of the bar at the beginning of a long hallway where the beautiful coffee boy with the amber eyes watched me in silence. I walked up the wooden planks as quietly as I could and entered what was almost a closet it was so tiny. It had a lock, and when I tried the hot water, it came out hot. *Bliss*. I was asleep long before the cantina downstairs closed and it was midafternoon the next day before I even stirred again.

If I had a higher power…*when* I had one…it was Hypnos, god of sleep, about half the time, and Thanatos his twin, god of peaceful death, the other half.

Fucking Greeks knew how to live.

* * *

When I got up, I just pulled on the jeans I'd worn the night before. Out of necessity, I only had a small bag with me, containing just a couple pairs of jeans, some T-shirts, socks, and, like, two pairs of underwear as a kind of homage to my mother. I wanted to check my bike, and I was tripping down the stairs and out the door before I effectively registered that anyone was in the bar. When I looked, Jim, his staff, and an odd assortment of others—about eight people altogether—sat at pulled-together tables, eating family-style from dishes of what looked like rice, beans, carnitas, and tortillas. It didn't look like the bar was open yet. I nodded to acknowledge them and went out the door, and when I came back after reassuring myself that my bike was intact, unticketed, and still where I'd left it, they were all staring at me.

"Come and eat, son," said Jim.

"Cooper," I said. I could see their eyes taking in my body with its webs of scars, tattoos, and the crisscross of whip marks like the faintest white fractures on flesh-toned earth. In the old days, I would've flashed an unrepentant grin, but these days I couldn't keep my eyes above anyone's knees to save my life.

"This is Alfred, my partner," said Jim, referring to an attractive man in his late thirties who looked at me with curious hazel eyes.

I held my hand out for him. "I'm just passing through," I said warily.

"Okay," he said, holding my hand in both of his and giving it an extra pat. "Have breakfast with us." He repeated Jim's invitation.

"Thank you. Let me get dressed," I said, but there were murmurs around the table.

"Don't bother dressing for us. Most of us are admiring the scenery." Jim winked.

I grimaced. "Lotta mileage." They smiled back.

It was a pleasure to sit down and eat, and the food was melt-in-your-mouth perfect. Thick, chewy homemade tortillas with pork carnitas, shoulder meat cooked in lard and spices until it was fall-apart delicious. Chunky salsa that defined the perfect balance between flavor and heat. Rice and beans any Mexican grandmother would kill to put on the table. Jim introduced me to Oscar and Tomas, who were apparently the cooks responsible, and I let them know how good I thought their food was. They seemed to swell with pride.

Someone passed me a big glass pitcher of what I thought was Bloody Mary so I started to pass it along when Jim said, "It's mix; there's no alcohol in it. I just like it with breakfast." I smiled to acknowledge his thoughtfulness, but I wasn't sure how I felt about everyone at the table knowing I didn't drink. Often that presented its own kind of challenge, particularly with men who didn't like to drink alone.

I looked around. No one seemed to be paying attention to the exchange between Jim and me, so I took the pitcher and filled a glass. I took a big swallow and it fucking blew my head off, the Tabasco flavor enhanced by a smoky burst of what could only be habanero pepper. Aw, shit, I was in tears, my face was probably red, and I couldn't breathe for a second. I fucking loved it. Culinary thrill seeking was one of the few avenues of harmless adventure open to me, and wherever I ended up these days, I found ways to indulge myself. A hand pounded on my back, and several of the men laughed.

They stopped laughing when they saw that I had no qualms about continuing to drink it, and then laughed even louder when I offered to suck them off so they could feel the burn for themselves, which earned me a mild reproof from Jim, who apparently had fiery firsthand experience with that very thing. When everyone stopped laughing, he leaned over to talk quietly to me.

"So, are you going to stick around Santo Ignacio for a while?" he asked.

I said, "I haven't thought about it. I was just passing through, but it seems...nice here." I didn't want to appear too eager. It *was* nice in Santo Ignacio, and I'd felt something here, both in this town and in this bar since the day before that I hadn't felt for a while. Acceptance, maybe, or simply peace.

"I can always use a hand around here in return for room and board," said Jim. "And if you play that violin, you could probably get tips. Summer's coming, and we get tourists. There's usually street performers on the boardwalk, and no law on the books as long as you're not out-and-out panhandling."

I thought about it. "Yeah. That might be...I could do that. What kind of help do you need around here? I've waited tables, cleaned, bounced. I'd prefer to avoid bartending." I knew how that sounded. Like I could be tempted. It wasn't that. The smell of hard alcohol makes me sicker than a pig, and to have drunks breathing on me... I couldn't do it.

"I understand," Jim said. No, he surely did not, but I wouldn't tell him that. "Actually, I could use a waiter sometimes—and someone to see that Oscar and Tomas don't kill each other. Do you have any experience in the kitchen?"

Did I ever. "Yes," I said. "I'm good with a knife." Oscar and Tomas exchanged glances. "Kitchen skills," I clarified. "Slice, dice, chop...food prep basics." They nodded, relieved.

"Good," said Jim. "I won't have to cut up all that crap for the bar." He'd made up his mind, even though I had yet to make up mine.

After breakfast, I prepared to start my first day of earning my keep. At the time, I knew I was willing to give it three days. I rarely stayed anywhere longer than that. Three days was always enough to know that I hadn't run far or fast enough and that my past was only minutes from catching up with me.

I called down the stairs and asked Jim if it would be okay for me to practice my violin. He said sure, the bar didn't open for about an hour, and if I knew any mariachi-style music I should be sure and drag it out. I knew "Las Mañanitas," "Cielito Lindo," "De Colores," and "La Bamba." In a pinch, I could listen to a CD and learn to play more. I pulled my violin out of its case, reacquainting myself with its heft and the feel of it against my skin. It had been almost a week, and like a lover, I held it for a while, tuning it up before I began to make it sing for me.

As soon as I began, I had the deep desire to descend, down the stairs, down to the basement if there was one, to play as deep inside the earth as I could, but I made myself get to work. I never let it fully rip anymore unless there wasn't another living soul around to hear me. I played gently, even sedately, where once I'd played as if possessed, until my teachers teased that my strings would catch fire.

This was the greatest of all my crimes, and every time I played I felt retribution on my neck like a breath. I had been given a real and apparently lasting gift by the gods, and I had thrown it away. Even though I carried my violin everywhere, it was only a reminder of what could have been. My fingers flew through the first of what would be a number of exercises, followed by classical pieces, followed by mariachi songs.

If I'd lost my gift, it would have been justice. If I'd lost my soul, my guilt would no longer haunt me. I still had both of those. I'd simply lost my humanity and everything else along with it that ever meant a shred of anything to me. And Santo Ignacio was as good a place as any to wallow in the knowledge of that.

Chapter Two

I went down the stairs that afternoon at five, as requested, to do whatever was required of me. Room and board. That was an answer to a prayer because even for a drifter like me, the road can feel long at times. I got to park my bike behind the bar and offload some more small things. I knew where I could find a coin-operated laundry.

Home sweet home.

I was asked to man the kitchen knives, the broom, the mop, the coffeemaker, the toilet brushes, and the hose out back when anyone puked. Simple enough. I would do this for four hours, and then if I chose, I could set up a tip jar and play mariachi music or whatever else I liked for the customers until ten, when the kitchen closed for everything but nachos and a DJ played dance music. On the weekends, I was to work the brunch crowds with music, and then take up my knives and cleaning tools, reversing the order.

Privately I believed it was merely a tacit way for Jim, the owner, to help me out. He didn't need me, which probably made me determined to be all the more useful. I was removing two rather large bags of trash when I literally bumped into the beautiful golden-eyed boy who'd served me coffee the night before. I apologized and murmured something inane, and he smiled at me with his expressive, open face, but said nothing. Later that evening, I was collecting the ashtrays from the patio for washing when I saw him yank his arm away from a customer.

Glancing sideways so he couldn't tell, I watched as he picked up some plates and placed them in one of those industrial gray tubs universal to busboys everywhere. He was collecting silverware and napkins and trash and moving from table to table wiping each down when the grabby drunk lurched up to follow him. What followed was some awkward thrashing and almost pushing that had me moving toward them. To catch his balance, the busboy had to drop the tub, and plates shattered on the concrete patio floor.

I cursed myself even as I began helping the boy pick up his shit. I had the broom out already because I was planning to sweep the patio after I got the ashtrays, and I used it to clean up the mess. As I was trying to get the smaller chunks of shattered porcelain I said, "I'm sorry. I'll help you clean this up. I saw that asshole bothering you; are you all right?"

The boy said nothing, just concentrated on picking up the silverware, scraping the bits of food off the concrete into his hands. I worried that he would cut himself.

"Here," I said slightly louder. "I'll get that, you go on ahead. I don't want you cut."

"Don't bother," said the man who caused the trouble in the first place. "It's not like he can hear you." The guy seemed to think this was funny and nudged his companion again. Fucking drunks. I'd been their patron *fucking* saint and I still couldn't get over how much I loathed them.

"What?" I asked, though I did it politely, which was a stretch.

"He's deaf, you asshole." Amber Eyes picked up the tub and left, not looking back.

Well. When a cosmic joke like that comes your way, you have to laugh. Amber Eyes was probably the first guy in three years who I saw in color, and he was deaf. And me? The only human language I had anymore was music.

* * *

I put the trash I'd collected off the patio floor into one of the big bins. It wasn't half full, so I didn't need to empty it yet. I was putting the broom and dustpan away when a hand came down on my shoulder. I turned to find the busboy there.

He was taller than me, which surprised me, but I didn't know why. Lots of people are taller than me. I'm not very big at five feet ten. Where I have muscles, partly because I used to play a lot of sports and partly because I burn off energy by exercising whenever I can't sleep—which is all the time—I was bulkier. Because of that I'd kind of assumed, from a distance, that I would be bigger. He was tall enough that I had to look up to see into those eyes, and right then they were just looking at me, with nothing in them.

"Thank you for helping me," he said, using the most utterly unmusical voice I'd ever heard and his hands. It was as if he couldn't talk without using both. Couldn't or wouldn't. I detected a hint of something defiant in the way he looked at me.

"You're welcome," I said. My turn to leave. Whatever the hell else I was getting into here, I didn't want to get into this.

A hand caught my shoulder and he turned me around, his grip surprisingly strong for such a slender man. "My name is Shawn," he signed and said.

"Cooper," I said, and already I was doing that careful thing, talking louder, exaggerating my pronunciation, and I hated myself for it.

"Hooper?" he asked, his fine eyes curious under a V of furrowed brows.

"Cooper," I said. I made a *C* with my hand because, yeah, I knew what a *C* looked like if I thought about it.

He nodded. "Cooper." Then smiled. Oh shit, he had a smile that...*dazzled.* I turned away and this time he didn't pull me back.

After I finished cutting up the rest of the bar fruit, I was free to play my violin for tips. I didn't kid myself as I walked up the stairs to my room to clean up. The men downstairs eating nachos would rather be watching the ballgame. In the restaurant part of the bar, there were a few couples eating at tables. If it sucked, and if everything went to hell, I could always play on the boardwalk on the weekend and make enough to get to the next town. The secret of my success was substantially lowered expectation.

I rosined up my bow, a ritual of sorts for me, as I scanned the smallish crowd. Jim turned off the overhead music, but the television over the bar still played the game. I began by playing "Las Mañanitas" for a man who was having a birthday party. His friends and the waiters sang; even Oscar came out to do the honors. After that, I passed a pleasant enough hour wandering between the restaurant, bar, and patio until it was time to push back the tables and set up a makeshift dance floor. I wasn't even sure that was legal, but here in St. Nacho's, as everyone in the bar referred to the town, rules didn't seem to have the bite they did in the world beyond.

Already I found myself slowing down to the pace of this sleepy town. I wondered how it was during summer, or even on weekends. I hadn't wondered about a town in a long time. Mostly, I just wanted to move on. I made close to twenty-five bucks in tips, and since I didn't have to pay for room and board, I felt rich.

Over and over I told myself not to sweat the details. The guy with the warm brown eyes was just a guy, and this was just another gig. In three days, four tops, I'd be heading out again. But then I got to know Jim and his lover, Alfred, pretty well the next day over breakfast. It turned out Alfred played the cello, and we bonded over being orchestra geeks in high school. That I didn't mention fucking up Juilliard wasn't really lying, I told myself; it was just that it was a long story, a long time ago, and it always went a long way toward ruining any relationship I had with serious musicians. It gets tiresome hearing that I'm too stupid to live.

Mostly I enjoyed my second day in the kitchen with Oscar and Tomas. They worked seamlessly together and still managed to argue the entire time. Tomas inexplicably called Oscar *precioso* snidely when he was angry, and just as strangely Oscar called Tomas *pendejo* when he felt tender toward him.

They gestured threateningly at each other all day long with big spoons because on my first day I'd hidden their chef's knives. They were quirky and worked well with each other, and the third morning I was there they made chilaquiles that were so good I thought I'd died and gone to heaven. I realized that morning that most of the people who worked at Nacho's ate breakfast there at around one in the afternoon, except for Shawn, the busboy, because he had classes at the junior college in the early part of the day Monday through Thursday. Also, it seemed, because his friends didn't like it.

Watching him, I wondered if I could survive in a world without sound, what it would mean to me to lose my hearing. It brought to mind Beethoven, because I had often pretended I was him when I was a kid. I used to imagine losing my ability to hear myself play the violin, going deaf until finally it was gone altogether. I thought if that happened I would disintegrate on the spot. Not out of sadness, because mostly it wasn't about my love affair with music, but because it was the last thing that tied me to any kind of self-concept. Music left me behind because I was a whore, but still I waited at the figurative window of my consciousness for it to return.

I splashed water on my face. Jim let me know where I could get some supplies and cigarettes. I was out of laundry detergent; being forced to travel light meant I could only buy the dispensable boxes or really small bottles. I needed soap. The soap in Jim's shower smelled like flowers, and I could smell it on myself hours after I'd used it.

I was walking back from the store with my plastic bag swinging from my arm, when I heard feet running toward me. When a hand grabbed my shoulder from behind, I overreacted, dropping my bag and spinning around the opposite direction to shake it off and loom a little. Even though I wasn't really tall, I had the tats and the piercings, and I could be intimidating. The last three years had made me hard. I knew my eyes looked at the world through a haze of pain, and worse, remorse. My own mother had found me frightening the last time I saw her. When I turned and stood to my full height, I realized the hand that caught at me belonged to Shawn, and I had definitely surprised him. He had been standing outside the convenience store with a group of his friends. They looked concerned; one was walking over to meet what he perceived to be a threat. I shook my head.

"Hi, Shawn," I said, relaxing. I picked up my bag again and grinned. "How are you?" I was feeling my way with this, not certain what to say, how to say it. I'd been told I mumble sometimes. I wanted to make myself as clear as possible, which was keeping me from acting naturally. And I hated it.

"Hi, Cooper," said Shawn, whose smile was still glowing inside me from the first time I'd seen it. His friend came up and threw an arm around him, but then let him go immediately to sign something to him. Unlike Shawn, he didn't use his voice, so I couldn't begin tell what he was saying. I kept my eyes on Shawn.

"This is Kevin," said Shawn. To Kevin he added, "Cooper works at Nacho's."

Kevin seemed to want to say something, but just took Shawn's hand in his and walked him back to the group of men and women he'd been standing with. They all signed, I saw, their beautiful hands fluttering their words into the air. I thought it looked like birds flying. Shawn was the most vivid of all, and he was the only one who spoke out loud.

He eyed me a little as he said, "He's nice. He plays the violin."

I grinned and turned away. Time to move on. Shawn's gang was made up of people who shared a life like his. I knew the deaf community in the town where I grew up was insular and had its own social hierarchy. They were differently abled, and a man who made his life by his ears wouldn't exactly be necessary or welcomed into their world.

I found my way back to Nacho's and up into my small studio there. Somehow, with these four bare walls around me, I felt safer than I had in three years. It was a sanctuary of sorts and made me think I needed to find St. Ignatius and do whatever it is you do for saints. I just wanted to stay out of the harsh glare of public scrutiny, do my job, and then fade away like a sigh when it came time to relocate.

It wasn't until that evening that I realized I'd blown the whole anonymity gig completely and that Shawn would inadvertently play a part in making me the center of controversy in sleepy St. Nacho's.

I was playing "De Colores," a mariachi tune as classic as margaritas on the fifth of May, when Shawn, who had the night off, and all his friends came in. Really, it was a quiet Thursday night at the bar, sometime between the dinner rush and the dancing that would follow when ten o'clock rolled around. I was beginning to enjoy this—the hour when I could play and chat with people I wouldn't call friends, but acquaintances. They listened with enthusiasm, a lot of them, because they'd never had anyone play just for them. The old fancy French restaurant staple of a violinist who played romantic music for a table was as foreign a concept in St. Nacho's as…well…a fancy French restaurant. I could already hear the difference the practice was making in the way I played, and I wasn't immune to the siren's song of my talent. I was getting better.

When Shawn came into the bar with his friends, he immediately sat the group at a table on the patio where I was playing and went to get them a round of drinks. He had three men and two girls with him. Their little party was so lively; they caught every eye in the place. Shawn returned and Kevin put a protective hand on the back of his chair. He and Shawn began to talk, and I saw a lot of glances headed my way. Kevin's looked a little frosty, and I wasn't surprised. He kept a hand on Shawn, or his chair, the entire time. Shawn even knocked it off a couple of times, but Kevin simply put it back surreptitiously when he wasn't paying attention.

Shawn waved at me and I gestured back with the neck of my violin without interrupting the piece. He and Kevin engaged in some sort of discussion. They all looked like passionate debates, and he scooted his chair away from Kevin's a little. Then Shawn smiled at me with the kind of smile that usually meant leaving town. And from the way Kevin stared at his profile, I saw I was right. Whatever they were saying, I would not be staying in St. Nacho's long enough to find out.

I turned and worked the tables in the opposite corner, deliberately. When it comes to a smile like the one on Shawn's face, I had to say, I was not immune to its charm. It spoke to me of summer and liking a boy because he helped you off the ground when another one shoved you. It reminded me of music camp, pancake breakfasts, cold lemonade, and playing in the orchestra at the Mall of America and going on an amusement park ride with the first chair cello, only to find out that he wanted to kiss me as badly as I wanted to kiss him. It was an open, curious smile, free of guile, which I could not even look at for its brightness and its hope.

Then suddenly, he was standing right before me, having tired of trying to get my attention any other way, and between songs I sighed and smiled back. He held out a beer as an offering, and I shook my head and declined, telling him firmly that I did not drink.

Wide, curious eyes that told me nothing met mine. "Iced tea?" he asked, carefully signing and speaking the words.

I nodded. He left to get me a glass and brought sweetener and lemon back with it on a saucer. "Play for me," he said. "I'll watch." He indicated the violin.

What devil possessed me, I couldn't say, but perhaps the simple troublemaker that was my constant companion made me take his hand and place it on the bottom of my violin as I began to play "La Habanera," from *Carmen*. His eyes widened, and he jerked his hand back completely as if it burned when I played the first few notes. Kevin leaped to his feet.

Oh, yeah. I'm a fucking Venus flytrap, all right. A man-eater.

Shawn motioned to Kevin to sit, adding, "Just chill, Kevin. It tickled is all," in his unmusical voice, and he replaced his hand, feeling the music through his fingers. I happen to know, because I play the thing all the time, that you can feel the difference between the high notes and the low. You can feel the violin tremble with my vibrato. You can feel both the inclination and the emotion of a musical piece by placing your hand on the side of the instrument, even if you're locked inside a soundproof box. Its voice carries in waves, like yours and like mine, and Shawn could feel my voice, my true voice, through his fingertips as I played my violin for him.

The last thing I expected was for him to understand this, but curse me for the idiot that I am, he *did* understand, perhaps too well. It was in his attitude. It was in his posture. But mostly it was in his eyes as they met mine, and he once again smiled. At me.

For the first time in ten years, my fingers lost their nerve. Or rather, I lost my concentration, and my violin sounded like a cat hitting a wall or a needle scratching across a record as the world stopped on an imaginary point in space. Silence hung thickly in the air as we stared at each other. I tried to return his smile, but couldn't find one that wasn't so used it was completely unworthy. I didn't have a fresh one and neither could I create a new one. I didn't have one to share with nice boys anymore.

Had Shawn shoved me out the door and up against the wall, or better, to my knees, I would have known just what to do. I laughed off my inability to play, made some kind of joke, and I took a long sip of my tea, unsweetened as penance for my sins, to buy myself time to think. Then I returned to "La Habanera," finishing my night out in the cantina with that piece. Shawn was back in his seat, looking at me thoughtfully, but I didn't let him have my eyes again.

Chapter Three

Later, I took my violin and my tips and went up the stairs to my room. I passed a long and sleepless night for which my muscles paid the eventual price, and I finally drifted off, exhausted, at six a.m. after about four hundred sit-ups and an uncounted number of push-ups.

I dragged myself to breakfast and found Shawn sitting at the table with the group I was accustomed, now, to consider my usual breakfast companions. It was awkward, in that I was trying to avoid him without making it obvious, and he was obviously trying to get my attention. I found my sanity in cataloging all the places that I couldn't look. That I couldn't look in Shawn's eyes was a given. He had a peculiar sensitivity to him, an ability to strip me bare of all my defenses. I also couldn't look at his mobile mouth, or his hands, as they combined to communicate everything that I could read in his eyes.

"Why don't you like me?" he asked bluntly, following me as I left the table to bus my own dishes. He caught hold of my shoulder and once again spun me to face him. "I can tell you avoid speaking to me."

"I do not," I said, looking over his head a little, a trick I use sometimes when I'm not willing to engage in any kind of eye contact.

"Liar," he said, but made the international sign *L* on his forehead for loser. "Is it because I'm deaf?"

"Of course not," I said, neatly caught, because I looked into his eyes then. Which looked triumphant.

"I want to be your friend," he said.

"I don't need friends."

"Yes, you do." He sighed, somehow, with his hands, and it was endearing, if annoying. "You need friends. But you push them away."

"I do not need friends," I said again. "I move on quickly. I don't have time."

He reached out and flicked me on the forehead, hard, and it hurt. I was rubbing the spot when he said, "I am your friend. Fuck you." Well. You can't argue with that. I couldn't help grinning.

"Fuck you back!" I said, knowing my fairish skin would have a loser bruise in the middle of my forehead soon. Shawn smiled that arresting smile again. I looked away. That hand came back out as soon as I did and caught my chin, forcing me to look at him. I flinched. I'm not proud of it.

"*I am your friend*," he said again.

I forced myself. "Thank you," I said, accompanying it with the one and only bit of sign language I knew, from somewhere, probably preschool. My hand to my mouth, and then down, palm up.

I got a rough hug for that, and then he left me alone. I decided to go out to the beach for a smoke, and Oscar, the other smoker from our little kitchen trio, joined me.

I found it entertaining that Oscar was beginning to include me in his little family, calling me *m'hijo*, and giving me a hard time about Shawn.

"Why you gotta act like that with Shawn, bro?" he asked me when he lit up. "He only wants to be friendly. He's like a puppy, man. You don't kick a puppy away for being nice."

"I'm just not into that," I said, giving him as wide a berth as I could while still sitting next to him on the wall. "I don't go around making friends. I move around too much. Saves hurt feelings."

"Whose, m'hijo, his or yours?" He gestured with his cigarette toward me. "I get you; you're a guy who doesn't stay in one place too long. But St. Nacho's? It can kind of capture you, even if you like moving on. It can't hurt having a friend here."

Oh, yeah, it can. "I'll think about it." I didn't really think about much else anyway, damn him. "I just like to keep it loose, you know?"

"I know." He tossed his butt on the ground and stomped it before picking it up again and tossing it into the trash. "I'm just saying…"

He left me there, stewing. I sat on the wall holding my crushed out butt in my hand. St. Nacho's kind of did that to you. You crushed your butt and held it, then threw it into a trash can. You didn't want to mess things up. Already I was regretting buying the sixteen-ounce bottle of laundry soap. I hoped it wouldn't break open in my duffel when I ran away from this place.

A body sat next to me on the wall, facing in the opposite direction. Shawn leaned back a little, his irrepressible grin in place as usual. He was silent for some time.

I already felt a kind of contentment sitting there with him. I could count on one hand the number of people in my entire life that I had endured a comfortable silence with. Shawn made number four.

"Pretty," he said finally, referring, I guess, to the day.

I didn't reply. He was turned away and wouldn't have heard.

"I want to listen to you play again," he said finally. "I want to hear it with my hands. I can feel music; I like it."

I smiled at him. "Okay." Shawn slapped a cell phone into my hands and closed my fingers around it.

"I borrowed this," he said. "'Cause I want to understand when you talk." He held up his own telephone. He took the one he'd given me back and scrolled around until he found the contact setup menu, then keyed in some numbers. "You want to talk to me? Text." He showed me where he'd added "Shawn" to the contact menu.

It wasn't that I didn't know how to use a cell phone. I just didn't own one. It's not like I had a place to send the bill. *Or anyone I wanted to talk to.* Remembering Oscar's comments not moments before, I bit back a sarcastic reply and took the phone from him.

I tried the phone experimentally. *How come you talk so well?* I typed, then sent.

Talk? Shawn replied using his phone. I saw possibilities with this. It would make it easier to avoid talking louder and miming everything I would say.

With your voice, I typed. *No one else does that.*

"I wasn't born deaf," he said. "I had bacterial meningitis when I was four years old. There was a complication and I had an almost fatal reaction to the antibiotic they used. I can remember talking, and it was something I could work on with teachers."

I see, I typed. *Do you remember music?*

He nodded. "What did you play last night?"

I bent my head to the phone's screen and texted, *It was called La Habanera, from Carmen, by Bizet.*

"Then tonight. 'La Habanera,'" he said, and tried to show me how to do tonight with my fingers. "You have a musician's hands. You should learn to sign."

I smiled but I doubt he thought I meant it. I didn't really. *I am lucky people understand when I talk*, I texted, thinking it was a good thing the phone had a computer-style keyboard. Our conversations were going to last hours at this rate.

"You do fine." He looked at me from under his lashes. "I understand you."

I realized that in silence lay safety, so I said nothing. My hands were still. It was when we talked that I felt uncomfortable. He relaxed his shoulders, and I could tell that, like me, he was allowing the sun to warm him.

"I find you attractive," he said, without using his hands. "I think you know that."

He looked at me, and I *couldn't* say anything.

He smiled a smile that didn't quite reach his eyes. "I wanted you to know anyway." He held a hand up when I started to text something. "I'm older than I look and I'm out and proud." He jumped down from the wall. "Just thought you should know."

Shawn left to go back in. It wasn't long after that when Kevin picked him up in a car, presumably to take him to class. I was still sitting on the wall when they drove out of sight.

I knew what to think then, and I thought it. Thought it and *thought it* and held it in my mind, but still, when night fell, I was there, my violin ready, to play for Shawn. After I was done with my chores, my hands smelled like garlic and onion and lemon. I washed with dishwashing soap to get the oils off. The scent was next to impossible to remove. I went upstairs and changed from the clothes I was wearing since I definitely didn't need the remains of my day job on my violin. At least, that's what I told myself. That I checked my look in the tiny mirror in my studio bathroom wasn't unintentional, and I even found myself staring back a little, wondering whether I should shave.

I started in the cantina itself, entertaining the couples there, doing a birthday song or two, playing some moody sentimental songs and mariachi favorites. Shawn wasn't in the house, and I relaxed into that thought, partly because I was glad, and partly because I was disappointed. I closed my eyes and played "Cielito Lindo" from somewhere deep in my memory, on autopilot, and thought about Shawn. It wasn't his day to work; he hadn't been there all afternoon. It was unlikely that he'd want to spend his day off at the very restaurant where he bused tables. It also didn't seem likely that Kevin, who had some sort of prior relationship with him, would want to spend the evening here either.

As if my thoughts conjured him, Shawn entered the bar with his friends. They took the same table on the patio they'd taken the evening before, and this time Kevin went off and got drinks. Shawn waved at me. I waved back with the neck of my violin. One of the men at the table where I was playing gave me a buck and asked me to play "Happy Birthday" for his boyfriend. I ended up playing both "Happy Birthday" and "Las Mañanitas" and moved on. Someone wanted to hear something more modern, and I searched my brain until I came up with "Sex and Candy," a Marcy Playground song I'd been rather fond of at one time. I played it as I walked around the tables, smiling and nodding at the customers. I knew how to do this.

After my song was over, I turned, and right behind me, as if he were waiting for me, was Shawn. I held my violin to my side.

"You said you would play 'La Habanera' for me," he said. "I'm waiting; it's tonight." He made the little gesture that said tonight with his hands.

I put my violin under my chin and played. I didn't have to place his hand on it this time; tentatively at first, but then with more certainty, he pressed his fingers to the underside of the instrument while I played. At first I found myself trying to look everywhere but at him, but it was hopeless. I couldn't help it; I wanted those eyes. I wanted to see what he was thinking. And I could. He was that transparent. He smiled a half smile as his body began to rock to the rhythm of the music, which, of course, was a dance. Time passed and we found ourselves swaying back and forth to the earthy melody until I was done. He clapped like a delighted child.

"I could feel it. Felt the rhythm," he said, thumping his chest in a rhythm as though he were listening to it. "I feel sound."

"I see," I said.

"We are all performers." He gestured to his group. "We sing."

Something on my face must have shown my disbelief, because he made a gesture at me and said, "Ear snob," and his friends signed in agreement.

"Do you know the song 'You Raise Me Up'?" asked Shawn.

I nodded. If I hadn't played that in about three-dozen weddings and at least as many graduations, I hadn't played it at all. I'd played it for my own sister's college graduation party.

Shawn motioned to Kevin, who went to the equipment that the DJ would be using later that night and started pressing buttons. I looked to Jim to see if he knew the kid was fooling with his sound system. When I got his attention, he flicked a glance at Kevin and then shrugged as if to say, "No sweat." I guessed this might not be the first time they'd done this.

Shawn nodded to his friends and stood talking to them for a few minutes. They arranged themselves in a semicircle, and I didn't know what to expect. Some of the other patrons gathered round. Shawn nodded to Kevin, who started the music and turned it up loud. The song had been made famous by Josh Groban, but I had originally found it in music school and liked it because it was a kissing cousin of "Londonderry Air." Shawn and his friends began to interpret the lyrics in American Sign Language, but more, they danced the words. It's a pretty but bland song, the lyrics the kind to guarantee shimmering eyes at a gooey, emotional wedding. Great song for the dance with Dad, I had always thought a little cynically.

Yet watching Shawn and his friends sing it, their lovely hands moving in both rhythm and harmony was so beautiful no words could really describe it. It was visually musical in a way I could never have expressed. I found watching them "sing" transcended my preconceived notions of what music was and wasn't. For a man who had lived all his life by his ears, I found myself rethinking my world. Mostly I watched Shawn, who seemed incandescent and radiated warmth to me, even though like the sun, he might as well have been ninety-three million miles away.

I guess I should have expected Shawn to follow me to my room afterward, except I thought Kevin wouldn't allow it. I was getting out of the shower when I heard the knock at my door. I really *was* surprised to find Shawn standing there.

"Hey," he said, taking in the fact that I only had a towel around my waist.

"Hey," I said, not opening the door to him. I kept my body in the way, blocking both the entrance and the view into the spartan little room.

"I came to say thank you," he said.

"You're welcome." At least I would make this difficult.

"I want to come in." His hand came up to smooth my wet hair behind an ear. "I like your tattoo." He pointed at the fetish tattoo I'd gotten years before, a heart with a whip sort of strangling it.

"Look," I said, trying to make my words visible, "you seem like a nice guy…"

He pushed my chest, and suddenly, he was in the apartment, closing the door behind him.

"Do I?" he asked, and it was as if he were two different people. "Do I seem like a nice guy to you?" He continued to touch me, and now he was running his thumb over the piercing in my eyebrow.

I think my eyebrows took off somewhere over my head. Warm brown eyes watched me, waiting for me to say something. He was sort of grinning, as though he were laughing at me.

"Yeah," I said. "Nice guy." Whatever he was doing to unbalance me was just that. I knew he was nice. The way my mother used nice when I was a kid: Don't touch that, it's not nice; be nice; play nice; he's a nice boy, the opposite of which was always the implied *nasty*.

Shawn was not a nasty boy. But I was.

I fell to my knees and began unbuckling his belt. He jumped back a little, clearly primed and ready but not for the speed at which things were progressing between us. My towel fell off and puddled on the floor. I yanked hard on the button at the top of his jeans.

"Oh, hey!" He gave a little yelp. I rubbed at his cock behind his zipper. I was careful in case he wore no underwear, but found he did. I unzipped him and pulled his shorts down to get a good look. He was hard and huge, his cock thudding into my hands, leaving a wet trail behind. He'd obviously been looking forward to something happening between us, and I really couldn't say I blamed him. I was too. I gave the underside of his dick an experimental lick and held my hand out for a condom.

"Latex?" I asked, looking up. He seemed shocked. His hands trembled as he reached for his wallet. "Condom?" I asked, trying to mouth the word clearly.

"I have one," he said.

"Only one?" I held up one finger as a question. I had some, but being a son of a bitch didn't require that I mention that.

"Yes," he said, stroking my hair tentatively. He was looking at me, but I had the advantage—I didn't have to watch him to hear him and I took it.

"Okay then." I got up and walked over to the bed, got on all fours, and looked back at him. I don't know what my plan was. I'm not sure I had one. "Come here." I crooked my finger.

Shawn said nothing and the silence kind of drew out between us as I continued to look at him over my shoulder. I could read his open face. Then the coin dropped for him on what I wanted and how I wanted it. I could see the exact moment when he made up his mind to give it to me. He dropped his trousers and kicked them off, and lurched up behind me on the spongy bed. He slapped me so hard on the ass that it stung, then leaned over and spit—which I had to give him credit for—into my hole like a porn star and started working me. Moments later, he put on his condom and entered me. He caught my forehead in his hand and pulled me back on him so he could grab my cock with his free hand and still keep his balance. He pounded me and worked my cock and then bit me and came.

So did I.

If someone asked me for the definition of hoist with my own petard, right then I would have given him an autographed picture. Shawn pulled me to him hard and licked where he'd bitten before we collapsed in a sweaty heap on the bed.

Without thinking, I said, "You've done this before." He tightened the arm over my waist.

"Save it," he said. "Unless I can see your lips, you're an inflatable doll." He removed the condom and tied it before making the shot right into the wastebasket across the small room for three points. I could feel his muscles relax even though mine remained frozen. Eventually, although I had no idea how long it took, he drifted off to sleep. I could feel his deep, even breathing, and heard a subtle snore.

Carefully, I turned around to look at him. *Crap*, he was gorgeous. He had high cheekbones and eyebrows that sort of feathered over large, deep-set eyes. His mouth was a wet dream, thick and luscious, kissable and bitable, slightly open and relaxed. I didn't dare touch him.

I slid cautiously off the bed and made my way to the shower, where I turned the water on as hot as I could stand it and let it wash over me. I tried not to feel as though I'd cheated myself, and Shawn, because there wasn't anything more I could really give him. I couldn't decide whether or not I wanted him to be there when I got back to bed, but he was. As I drifted off to sleep, I wondered if he'd still be there in the morning, but he wasn't. And for the first time in years, maybe I got exactly what I'd asked for, but not at all what I wanted.

Chapter Four

Apparently on Saturdays Shawn joined the rest of the staff for breakfast. I was distracted by Oscar's pointed looks in my direction and Shawn's rather disturbing determination to ignore me. For once, it wasn't me avoiding eye contact. It was pointless to worry about it; it was Saturday and I was certain I would be moving on by Sunday afternoon. I already had seventy-five dollars in tips, and if I slept outside I could go a long time on that. I bused my dishes and went to the convenience store for cigs. I saw Kevin when I was on my way back, driving Shawn someplace, probably not to school on a Saturday. As usual, they were in animated conversation, a term I hadn't given much thought to before I met them. It was a wonder they managed to keep enough hands on the wheel to steer the car, and a miracle that it didn't go skidding off the road. Shawn saw me but kept his eyes straight ahead. I felt like a shit, but I knew it was for the best.

When I got back to the bar, I thought I ought to tell Jim it was time for me to be moving on. Jim was getting ready to open and was checking his stock.

"What?" he asked. "I thought St. Nacho's was treating you pretty well." He stared me down.

"Yeah, well. I don't usually stay in one place too long." I know I mumbled.

"I wonder if you should rethink that."

I smiled. "Probably." The easiest thing to do when someone is lecturing is agree.

"Have you told Shawn?"

"I'll mention it next time I see him," I said, as though Jim hadn't seen Shawn follow me to my room last night.

Jim's eyebrows rose. "I kind of thought you guys got along."

"Sure," I said. "He's a good kid."

Jim barked out a laugh. "He gets that a lot." He picked up a bar towel and started wiping down surfaces, more I think to give himself something to do than because the counter was dirty. "Don't be fooled. He looks like an angel, doesn't he?"

"Hey," said Oscar, coming out of the kitchen. "Cooper, are you going to come get started? The trash can is calling." He crossed his arms.

"On it," I said over my shoulder before I turned back to Jim. "Look, I want to say thank you for everything you've done for me. I know you've gone out of your way to help me."

"I won't consider you gone until I see you ride away on that bike of yours, Cooper. I still say you ought to rethink St. Nacho's. It's a good slowing down spot."

"Who says I'm slowing down?" I replied with a smile that I didn't really feel. *I was slowing down*. And yet I felt the compulsion to speed up again, and it was hitting me hard.

"Cooper," Oscar said impatiently.

"Coming." I went to the kitchen and began my day.

By the time I was playing my violin that evening, I wasn't so sure about leaving. I originally thought Saturday would be crowded with weekenders, or that the dance crowd would push me along so they could get to the dancing faster. In fact, the opposite was true. Alfred was there with friends, and he brought his cello, and we played impromptu duets. The crowd requested classical pieces, and I laughed and played in a way that I hadn't since high school. I was playing for the fun of it. My case filled with paper money and change, and someone even left Lindt truffles in a little bag for me. I suspected Alfred of that; he seemed like the kind to sneak a treat to a friend.

Shawn didn't come in until almost time to push the tables back. He came with his pack, and I recall thinking they looked like a gang. They looked unhappy, and absurdly, the whole scene reminded me of *West Side Story*. There was a definite *us* and a definite *them*. I thought it had more to do with how Shawn and I had spent the night before than with anything I was doing right then.

Shawn came straight toward me when I finished the piece I was playing with Alfred. Kevin went to the soundboard again and cued up a CD.

"'La Habanera,'" he said. Just like that, with a challenge in his eyes.

Together, Shawn and Kevin began to dance. They tangoed through the first part of the music, a lovely, intensely exciting dance. Then they broke apart and Shawn began to sign, and *holy shit*, he was perfect. He signed the

English translation of the song—the rebellious bird, the gypsy child—all the while doing a captivating side-by-side dance with Kevin and flirtatiously looking over his shoulder at me.

When he came to the part when Carmen sings, "If you don't love me, I love you; if you don't love me, watch out!" he continued to watch me as he danced and "sang," and I couldn't take my eyes away. He sang with his hands and it was the most vibrant, erotic thing. Those hands had been on me, and his body fused with mine. I knew right then I wasn't leaving the next day.

I helped push the tables back and tried to melt into the crowd. Shawn sought me out. "Let's dance," he said, tugging at my hand. I held my violin case, and I wanted to put it away.

"I have to go," I said, holding it up so he could see.

"Okay." He pulled me toward the stairway and went up the stairs with me. I intended to put my case inside my room and stay there, but he pulled me to him as soon as we entered. I pushed him away.

"Come and dance with me," he said.

The lights were dim, and I wanted to make sure he could see me when we talked. I shook my head. "I don't think so."

"Why not?" he asked. "Do you have another date?" The lack of inflection in his voice always surprised me, but I was growing to like it. I don't know why; its very lack of musicality was a novelty in my world.

"Don't you?" I asked, gesturing to the door, hoping he'd understand what I meant.

"Kevin? No, I don't date Kevin. He tries to protect me from the big bad wolves. He thinks I'm nice too." Shawn grinned then, looking anything but nice.

I couldn't help but grin back. Nice boys didn't fuck like he did.

"Dance with me," he said. He removed a box from his jacket pocket; it had three-dozen condoms in it. From his other pocket he removed a large handful of flavored singles and a tube of lube. He tossed them down on the bed. After a minute he tossed off his jacket too. Like he knew he'd end up there.

"Taking a lot for granted," I said. I must have mumbled because he ignored me.

"Dance with me," he repeated. He held out his hand, and I took it. We went down the stairs together. Already the bass was throbbing. The DJ began scratching out a rhythm. I looked for his gang, and they were there, some dancing, Kevin still sitting, talking to one of the girls. He looked our way and then away again quickly, but not before I caught the annoyance that crossed his face.

After that, every move was foreplay, pure and simple. Our bodies found each other in the crush and we used every possible brush and touch to arouse one another. I was breathless with it. He was sweating. We came together like mercury for several songs.

"Water?" he shouted over the crowd, and I nodded. He left me standing there on the dance floor, hard as stone, and I watched as he walked away. Everything about him attracted me. He had a smooth, easy grace, a dancer's body, hands that spoke in eloquent flutterings, and a beautiful face. I was sure even the soles of his feet would make me hard.

The disco ball spun overhead, giving the room that giddy, timeless, strobe-lit club vibe. Shawn returned, sliding easily into me, and handed me the water. He had one of his own, and I watched him drink it, my gaze taking in his full lips and the way his throat moved as the water slid down it. My own mouth dropped open as I caught my breath. A drop escaped his lips as he pulled the bottle away and started to trickle down his chin, and before I thought about it, before I could stop myself, my tongue was there, capturing it. He reached a large hand out to cup my butt and pulled me into his groin. There was not a doubt in my mind that if I stayed there with him, rocking like that, hard against him, I'd come. He must have seen it in my eyes.

"Come on." He jerked me along toward the stairs. When we got there, Kevin was standing in the way, rippling with indignation. Shawn and Kevin had words, or signs, each agitated, and for once, Shawn wasn't speaking so I couldn't tell what was being said. Kevin finally ended the conversation by giving Shawn a hard shove on the chest with both hands. I stood next to Shawn with my arms crossed and put out a hand when Kevin pushed him. If Kevin did it again, he was going to have to get up off the ground afterward. He understood and stalked away. I couldn't help but glare at Shawn a little, and he wasn't any too happy either.

"Upstairs," he shouted over the music. "We can talk." Both of us knew that wasn't why we had been going upstairs in the first place. My room was at least a little quieter than the bar, and I opened the window and turned on a switch in the bathroom to light the bedroom a little. I opened and began to drink my water. I could feel Shawn behind me, getting closer. He radiated warmth and energy; I could feel it coming off of him in waves.

"Turn around," he said. I complied, and he pulled me to him to begin another dance. He was all physical, I realized. All motion, high octane, high energy. He liked to move and used his body for everything. Still swaying with me, he ran his hands through my hair, then over my face. I closed my eyes and just let him have me, let him play with my body in any way he wanted. He stroked, pushed, pulled, and spun me around in the small space. A hand on my ass held me firm for a while. I knew he wanted to kiss me, and I broke away, bringing the water bottle to my mouth, trying to make it look as natural and normal as I could. Trying to make it look like I wasn't avoiding his kiss.

He got his own water and took off his shirt. "Hot," he said, waving it to cool him in the small space.

"Oh, yeah," I agreed. "Hot." I smiled. He bussed me on the cheek for that, mostly because I turned at the last moment. I took off my own shirt. After that, it seemed like we just didn't need our jeans, and soon enough I was rocking against that hard body of Shawn's without any clothing on at all. He was magnificent and clothing just didn't do him justice. He moved like water, or something thick, like honey, and he was red hot against my cooling skin. I touched him everywhere, exploring, tasting, teasing, testing, until he caught my face and tried to kiss my mouth, to invade me there, and I turned my head away, had to, with force that became a struggle between us.

"I don't kiss," I said. I looked at his Adam's apple, waiting.

"You don't kiss," he repeated.

I had to look into his eyes. To make him see I was serious. "I don't kiss." We stared at each other for a long time. Finally, he nodded and caught me to him again.

"Like *Pretty Woman*," he said against my ear, then pulled back to look at me.

"What?" I asked him.

"The girl in that movie, the hooker. She didn't kiss," he said in that curiously flat voice of his. I never realized how much I depended on the inflection of someone's voice to get my bearings. With Shawn, I didn't have that to guide me so I was perpetually off course.

"Ah, I guess." I shrugged. "I didn't see the movie."

He grinned. He kept dancing with me but didn't press the kissing issue. If there was something right then I could describe later, something that struck me as being rare or new or vaguely disturbing, it was how completely at home I felt in Shawn's arms. How my body went to his, effortlessly, unconsciously, for pleasure in touch. How I savored every particular brush and rub and pull and play of our bodies against one another until he pulled me down with him on the bed and at last worked his way into me. By this time, we were both desperate; I pushed back off the headboard with both hands as he lifted my hips and dug into me, pounding me until I gasped in shock. He hooked one strong hand around my hips and used his free hand on my cock, and the next thing I knew, I was coming like a teenager, ribboning onto his chest, my chest, getting sticky, sweaty, and glued together as he sagged onto me after his own release. He crushed me to him, but didn't kiss me. When he moved to get rid of the condom, he went to the bathroom. He returned with a wet towel, dabbing us off and cooling our skin. It felt nice; I couldn't remember anyone ever doing that before.

I caught his hand as it swept by a nipple and gave it a squeeze. He smiled his angelic smile in return. He tossed the wet towel over onto the bathroom floor and curled up with me to sleep.

I didn't say anything. He was behind me, and he'd only feel the vibration, not hear the words. I didn't mind that so much anyway, because I had no idea what to say. His hand started at my hip and caressed me, sliding over my belly and settling across my chest, where it tightened, pulling me to him to hold me fast. I lifted a hand and interlocked my fingers with his. This was the single most intimate thing I'd done in five years.

It wasn't long after that we fell asleep, despite the music filling the room from downstairs. He and I woke up at different times through the night, always finding each other, straining together, and bringing each other off. I got to know the feel of him, the weight of him, the strength and taste and smell. He held me tightly in his arms, and when he needed to, he just got up and dressed. By then I belonged to him; I was property, and somehow he knew it. He only looked back once for reassurance that we both understood that before he left.

Chapter Five

When I came down at eight a.m. to start my day, Oscar and Tomas were already fighting in the kitchen. Jim just looked at me and smiled.

"I guess you'll be staying awhile," he said, giving me the once over. Alfred came up from behind him and rested a head on his shoulder.

"Yeah," I said.

"I thought you might reconsider," said Alfred.

"What's going on?" I asked, to change the subject.

"It's Sunday," said Jim, as if I'd asked what day it was. I was confused, until I saw Shawn dragging out a big sign that read, NACHO'S FAMOUS SUNDAY BRUNCH.

The sign had small laminated newspaper articles on it from as far away as the *San Francisco Chronicle* and the *Sacramento Bee* touting the "Best casual brunch on the West Coast," and "A terrific brunch for not a lot of bucks."

Sunday mornings were different at Nacho's because they served the brunch buffet-style, and this morning it was my job to see to the steam tables and make sure they were refreshed as needed. Both Jim and Alfred, who worked efficiently and cooperatively, joined Oscar and Tomas in the frantic kitchen. Eventually each of us got breakfast, taking turns while the others worked. It seemed that everyone in St. Nacho's, gay and straight, found their way to Nacho's for brunch on Sunday, and often they came with crowds of their out-of-town friends.

For a while, almost an hour and a half, I played the violin for the lively crowd, which was tanking up on cheap champagne and chasing it with fiery salsa. I probably got about a hundred dollars in tips during that hour and a half, almost as much as I had made the whole week.

By five in the afternoon, we had the aftermath of the brunch cleaned up and put away. Then everyone effectively had a night off because the club was closed on Sundays. I found myself a nice spot on the seawall, and I relaxed with a cigarette.

"I saw the people when you played." Shawn came up behind me and jumped up to sit. As he'd done before, he faced the opposite direction so he could study my face as we talked. His hand idly slid across my belly and onto my farthest hip, his thumb in the watch pocket of my jeans. "They looked really impressed. Are you that good?" he asked. He tapped my pocket where I kept the cell phone he'd loaned me, and I dutifully took it out.

Probably, I texted him. False humility wasn't one of my failings, and it didn't pay to lie about something he could easily check with any number of people.

"Do you ever go see plays?" he asked.

"I have," I said, carefully nodding.

"I have tickets for a play next Friday night in Santa Barbara. Will you come with me?" He grinned.

Are you asking me out on a date? I used the phone for that; it gave me something to do and kept me from looking into his eyes.

"Yep."

Thumb, thumb, thumb. *Can I think about it?* I felt myself turn red. Friday was a lifetime away.

"Yeah," he said. "Not too long, though." He took my cigarette away from me and brought it to his own lips. He took a drag and exhaled. I expected him to cough, but he didn't. He kissed my neck, where my ink was, and licked it lightly. "Got the night off?" he asked.

"Yep." I nodded. Inside I was smiling already, but I thought I ought to make him work for it a little.

"You going to make me ask?"

"Ask what?" I found myself miming my words. I hoped that would go away soon.

"If your ass belongs to me or not," he said roughly in my ear.

"It does." I nodded.

"Bring it." He jumped down off the wall. "We're going to Jim and Alfred's." I had little choice but to follow along. I took off after him, but he didn't look back. Jim and Alfred lived about a block away from the bar in a Victorian-style home that had been remodeled a number of times, and had frankly seen better days.

At one point, I suspected, the house hadn't had a bathroom indoors, because it had one off the kitchen that looked like someone cut a hole in the wall and just stuck it there. The wooden floor sagged just a little in the middle of the living room, but the big bay window looked out on the picturesque main street of St. Nacho's and its quaint mixture of woods and beach. It looked more like Oregon here than California, and I still had a hard time believing the luck that drew me here. It was a fact that I waited with my heart in my throat for my good fortune here to blow up in my face.

"Hey!" said Jim, coming down the stairs to the kitchen where Alfred was showing us around. Jim mixed me up a fiery Virgin Mary and then made a pitcher with booze for the three of them. He watched me carefully, I suspect, still thinking I wanted one. I'm sure he'd seen a thousand alcoholics come through his bar, both drinking and sober. I knew there was nothing in the world that could make me drink. But unless I told him how I knew that, he would always look at me the way he was looking right now, with a kind of considering and frank appraisal, as if he were readying himself for disappointment.

"Did you bring your violin?" asked Alfred.

"No," I said. "Was I supposed to? It's not a long walk; I can go get it."

Jim said, "Let the poor man have a night off, Al." He turned to me. "We're going to watch *The Grudge*." He nudged Alfred. "Scary movies and snuggling; hot chocolate and popcorn. This is a date," he warned.

Shawn came up behind me and put his arms around me. They brushed down my torso, and I leaned into him.

We gathered supplies, which included the ubiquitous chips and salsa, some homemade guacamole, and a big bowl of popcorn, which for a twist was topped with sugar and cinnamon like *buñuelos*. The cocoa had a cinnamon kick to it too, along with what I suspected was a hint of cayenne. Everything was good, spicy, and tasted even better on Shawn's lips than it did fresh. I wanted to remember the spicy scent on his breath, the way the movie made me move closer to him, and how the subtitles crawled across the screen and none of us paid it any mind after the first few seconds. Jim, Alfred, and I responded to the musical cues and noises that Shawn missed, so he often laughed when I jumped for what he imagined was no good reason. Visual cues made him startle, but by then, we'd already reacted.

It had probably been ten years since I'd had a night like that, watching movies with friends. Something scared me then, something that had nothing to do with the movie and everything to do with nice people, kindness, and getting too comfortable.

It made me want to leave. I got up, maybe a little quickly, but I knew they couldn't read the panic that was building in my heart. Shawn got up and followed me to the door. When we were once again in the briny night air I faced him.

Look, I typed into the phone with my face down, *If you're having a nice time, you don't have to leave. I can get home. Just because I'm calling it an early night doesn't mean*—He put his hands over mine and stopped me from texting.

"You talk too much," he said, grinning. He began to walk back to my place rather briskly, and I had to catch up.

"Long-legged bastard," I said out loud, knowing he couldn't hear me.

He put his arm around me, and said quite clearly, "When I'm touching you, I can feel that you're talking. I can also see you reflected in the windows of the cars parked on the street." He indicated the car we'd just passed.

Well. He *was* a clever one. I caught his arm so he faced me. "And do you have a crystal ball?" Could he read lips that well?

"Nope," he said, continuing to walk. "I don't need a crystal ball, I got these." He cupped himself, which made me laugh. He looked at me to see how I was taking it and laughed. I'd heard his laugh before, but it still surprised me. He laughed like a baby. Like air being moved through an accordion with no one playing it.

Jim said not to let your looks fool me, I texted. He read his phone with a V-shaped dip between his fine brows.

"My looks?"

Yeah, you look like an angel, I thumbed, still walking. I turned to find he'd stopped.

"You think I look like an angel?"

"I do, yes." I nodded. I walked back to where he stood. I was concerned I'd touched a sore spot with him, or hurt him in some way. He looked at me with something in his eyes I couldn't read. He smiled then, and it transformed him. He threw an arm back over my shoulder and started walking again, moving the both of us quickly until we were unlocking the door and rushing up the stairs. He threw me back against the wall outside the door to the little studio, on the narrow landing at the top of the stairs.

"Oh, fuck," he said, and it was kind of funny, hearing him swear like that, he just couldn't do it justice. "Come here, baby." He ground his hips into mine, pushing my hands above my head and holding them in one of his own while he got my belt buckle undone and my zipper down with his other hand. My cock bounced out into his hand, and he held it, his eyes on mine, asking. He began to move in for a kiss and I turned my head. My knees buckled a little from his hand on my balls.

"Key?" he asked, and I shook my head. He let me go and we tumbled together through the unlocked door. After that, everything that happened was a blur of sensation and a battle of wills. I wanted him inside me; he wanted to tease. He found my cock with his lips and used them to roll down a flavored condom. He sucked me off like I'd never been sucked—mouth everywhere, fingers questing, stroking me from the inside and the outside at the same time. I blew like a geyser, jerking and pulsing in his beautiful hands.

I wanted him to bury himself in me, but he pushed me to my knees, rolled a condom on his own dick, and fucked my mouth. I sucked him in until I was nose deep in his thatch of curly brown hair and he shot hard into the latex. He brought me to my feet after and rubbed his thumb across my lower lip. He leaned in again and I turned my head, but he found my lips anyway, chasing and finally trapping me against the side of the bed and the wall so that I couldn't turn any further. He teased my lips gently, mouth closed. As delicately as he would have kissed a baby's face, as tentative and shy as a kid in middle school. Heaven help me, a burning ball of pain closed my throat and I felt the sting of it gather in my eyes. I closed them.

Shawn pushed me to the mattress and held me. I didn't cry, but it was a near thing and we both knew it. I woke several times in the night, and every one of them surprised me. Finding Shawn beside me, the comfort of his chest against my back, his fingers interlaced with my own, was new. Everything seemed new. And I knew that if I couldn't find my balance here in St. Nacho's, I'd lose myself to the comfort and the tenderness of this. Then when I had to leave, as I had no doubt I would, the pain would kill me.

When I ran a curious finger down the side of Shawn's face, he woke and smiled sleepily. He no sooner saw me than he was on me and hard, reaching for a condom and seeking entrance. He faced me this time, and we made love looking at each other. Our silence blanketed us like fog. If nothing else, in that moment I wanted him to have everything I had to give, and inside myself I found things even I didn't know I had.

* * *

I woke up when I realized someone was pounding on my door. Shawn was oblivious. Catching the sheet and pulling it around myself toga-style, I got up and answered it, sure it couldn't be anything good.

It wasn't.

Kevin stomped to the bed angrily, his feet popping on the hardwood floor. He slapped Shawn's arm hard. Shawn jumped, shattered into wakefulness from a sound sleep.

"Hey!" I said, but of course they didn't hear me. They gestured at each other wildly, and while I couldn't say exactly what they were saying to each other because Shawn wasn't talking, I could see it was a litany of accusations and denials, guilt and remorse and recrimination. I wanted no part of that. I locked myself in the bathroom and turned on the shower. I told myself I would let them have the clash of the titans without me.

I was in the shower when a sound echoed off the tiles. I pulled the curtain aside to find Shawn standing in front of me, triumphantly holding a screwdriver and the doorknob. He tossed it onto the sink next to my towel and got in with me.

"Shawn," I said, holding a hand up.

"I handled it," he said, his eyes on my face.

"But…"

"I said I handled it. He wants me. I want you. End of story." He squeezed a blob of shampoo into his hand and started working it into my hair.

"Oh, damn, baby." I melted under those big, clever hands of his.

He kissed my forehead.

"But," I said, holding him so he could see I was serious. "Why?" I asked. "Why me? Why not Kevin?"

Shawn shrugged. "I don't know why not Kevin. I saw you, and right away I wanted you. I watched your eyes, watching me." He began to use his hands unconsciously, and I was reminded of how he looked when he spoke like that. "You have places in you that I've never seen, things I don't know." He cupped my face in his hands and kissed me, and in light of what he was saying, I let him. I opened my mouth and my heart and I kissed him back, cursing myself for a damned fool even as I did it.

"Shawn." I sighed.

"I don't know why it was you, but it was… It is. And it's more than just this," he said, grinding me a little. "Not that *this* is bad…"

"No," I gasped, shaking my head. "Not bad."

He went to kiss me again, and automatically, I turned away.

"I thought we were kissing now," he said, giving my shoulders a squeeze.

I turned back to him and gave him a kiss. Even to me, it seemed strained. Water rushed over us, between us. He rubbed circles on my ass.

"Are you going to talk to me about that?" he asked. Brown eyes blinked as water hit them. I wanted to put my forehead in the hollow if his throat and leave it there. Forever.

"Now?" I asked, and shook my head again.

"When?" He was still circling my back with his large hands, and I was melting under his touch. It's amazing how simple and clear everything feels when someone is touching you, and for me it had been so long.

"Later. With clothes on." I succumbed to the desire to lean in and be held, and he complied, enfolding me in what seemed like impossibly strong arms.

"Later," he said, before we melted into each other.

After lunch, Shawn caught my hand in his. I didn't know what his school schedule was, but it was Monday and he wasn't in class. I didn't know how old he was, or where he lived, or anything about is parents. I didn't know anything at all about the man who held my hands and sat before me on the beach, but I found myself telling him things I'd never told a living soul. Later I would realize that Santo Ignacio is just like that, a place to bring your shit and put it down.

I was sitting cross-legged on the beach, in the sand with Shawn, feeling the warmth of the sun as it tried to break through the marine layer. It was still a little cold, and I had gooseflesh under my T-shirt. Shawn caught my hands in his and rubbed briskly to warm them.

"So," I said, entirely uncomfortable with this.

"So," he repeated. He lifted my hand to his lips. "Why no kissing?" He prodded until I got out my phone, and then he made a show of opening his up.

I looked down a little. *Because I feel like a fucking idiot*, I typed carefully.

Shawn's brows rose and he snickered. "I see."

I pushed dry sand around with my foot, burying it. My fingers didn't really text all that easily, and I made a hundred small typos, going back to clear them up. *I used to drink a lot*, I sent. Then started again. *I mean A LOT. I was really young. I stopped suddenly. I did rehab. I learned things.* I didn't like what I'd learned, but I had learned. Patient brown eyes watched me. My thumbs were getting faster or I'd have had a nervous breakdown on the spot. *I've never done it sober.*

"You've never had sex sober," he said, still watching me with those amber-colored eyes.

"Yes." I nodded. "No. Well. I've had sex," I told him.

"But no kissing," he repeated. "No intimacy. But sex is okay." I felt like I was going through rehab again and my face was heating up. I tried to tamp it down.

My thumbs got serious. They seemed big on those tiny little buttons, and I resented my dexterity from playing the violin didn't come in more handy. *It's like a camera in my head or some eye watching*, I tried to explain. *Someone judging me, finding every flaw. Someone critical. I hear every noise. Everything goes in slow motion. I used to just fuck. Anyone. Like a machine. I'm not proud of it. I survived. I'm negative. Some people I knew aren't.*

He squeezed my hand, and smiled faintly.

I started another text. *I am used goods. I have no clue how to do this.* I shook my head.

"What?" asked Shawn.

I shrugged. *It's easy when someone uses me. Hard and fast. Hit and run. That's me now. I never slow down.* I admitted this into that impersonal machine, eyes down.

"Santo Ignacio slowing you down? I've heard it can be like that," he said. His mouth quirked into a shy smile.

Something's slowing me down, I typed. I looked up and got caught in his eyes.

Shawn wrapped those big hands around my face, and I could feel the many rings he wore against my warming skin. "You've gotta know you are one sexy bastard, right?"

"I don't know. I don't get complaints much," I said, hoping he could read my lips because he wasn't letting me put my head down to type. I hated this. I could feel myself tensing up all over. "I don't usually wait for reviews."

He reached over and pushed my chest hard enough that I had to lean back on my elbows to keep my balance. I straightened my legs out front and he threw one of his over. "Biker boy wows the hearing impaired," he said, leaning in to kiss me. "Biker boy rocks the house." He touched his lips to mine. "Shawn Fielding rates biker cock number one with a bullet." He kissed me hard, and I kind of liked it.

Hey, I typed when he let me go. *That's your last name?*

He slipped his arms around me. "What's yours?"

Wyatt, I texted. I heard sand crunch and shift behind me, and I turned to see Jim backlit by the sun as it tried to come through the clouds.

"Hey, if you guys are through getting sand in your unmentionables, I could use some help back at the bar," he said. I got up and helped Shawn to his feet. We dusted ourselves off. I'm sure I looked like a guilty kid.

"Coming," I said. Shawn and I walked back with him to Nacho's, holding hands.

Chapter Six

Santo Ignacio was changing me. I could feel it in the way I held my body more relaxed and my jaw less rigid. Often, my hands were loose at my sides. I smiled a number of times each day, and at first when this happened, people asked me about it. It felt like using unfamiliar muscles for a few times until my face could get it right. Coworkers and regular customers who had seen me off and on for a week remarked that I seemed to be getting into the spirit of the place. At first I fought it, afraid of losing my edge. I didn't want to get lulled into a false complacency and have to move on, merging back onto the endless interstate where places like Santo Ignacio were a dim and civilized memory.

I felt particularly overwhelmed one night when Shawn came by Nacho's after I finished playing and was helping to push the tables out of the way.

"Hey." He caught my eye and winked, holding up a pint of Chubby Hubby ice cream and a couple of spoons. We walked to the beach together and ate out of the carton on the sand.

I smiled when he tried to feed me off his spoon, but at the same time a part of me wanted to fight. "Don't feed me," I said, jerking my head back. He didn't hear me because something had caught his attention farther down the beach, so he continued to hold the spoon near my face. I shoved his hand away, less than pleased.

"What?" he asked, a little shocked.

"You don't have to feed me," I said, holding up my spoon.

"Okay," he said warily.

I stabbed the spoon into the softening ice cream and flopped onto my back. The sky was inky but there were no stars. The moon was half full and trying to find a way to shine through fast-moving clouds. After finishing the ice cream, Shawn lay down beside me and watched the clouds too.

He interlaced his fingers with mine, and we lay there for quite some time. "Is this what it's supposed to be like?" I asked, forgetting that if he wasn't watching my mouth he couldn't hear me. The silence bore down on me, comfortable, familiar. The solid connection of our hands began to mean something to me, the ice cream forgotten. I turned to him and put my head on his chest so I could feel his heart beat. His hand came over to stroke my hair, and I felt contentment in his touch.

"I have always lived in silence, but I've never felt alone," he remarked.

* * *

I wanted to stay there forever, but Shawn was restless and wanted to walk. We held hands and ambled along the beach, getting our feet wet and holding our shoes. I don't think I'd ever done such a thing. Everything I did felt entirely unfamiliar, and it was so sharp with new emotions and sensations it was painful. I swallowed hard and followed along.

Sometimes something simple and relatively harmless would break over me like a wave. It was like that the night we ate the ice cream. We returned to my room and he got to his knees and took me into his mouth, so determined to give me pleasure that I started to cry. I was grateful that he had no idea. By the time he looked at me again I was over it. This could not last. Sooner or later even this respite, this brief time in Santo Ignacio would end, and with it, whatever it was I had with Shawn. I didn't want to get too used to it. I couldn't.

* * *

Friday came, and I got the evening off to go to the play with Shawn. I can honestly say that I don't actually remember ever going out on a date. Not like a real date, where a guy asked me out. I'd probably forgotten more of my life than I remembered, anyway.

I was completely floored when Shawn showed up in a car to take me out. I stared unmoving from the window of the studio, looking down from the bathroom onto the street below, and I felt frozen in place. Rigid. I couldn't move. In that moment I realized I'd never told him I didn't ride in cars. It had never come up. Everything in town was within walking distance, and I had my bike. I'd even gotten an extra helmet from Oscar for the evening assuming we'd take that.

He appeared to be waiting for me to come down. I took the stairs slowly, trying to think.

"Hey there," said Jim. "Shawn's outside." I headed past him without saying anything.

Shawn was waving. "Sorry I'm late," he said. He bussed me on the cheek and held the door open. I wasn't really dressed like he was, but he said nothing. I looked at the car. This would be the first time in three and a half years. I took a deep breath. He took my elbow impatiently, and I yanked it away. I didn't need help to get into a car. I swallowed and sat on the seat, sliding in. It was a Toyota Camry, a white nineties model, but well cared for. I buckled the lap belt, knowing the shoulder restraint would travel along a mechanism and pull tight around my chest as soon as Shawn keyed the ignition. I tried as hard as I could to breathe deeply and evenly. I told myself I could do it. I told myself it was a car, not a truck. I told myself it was Shawn driving, not...

"What's with your face?" Shawn asked. I turned to him, pasting a smile on that I didn't feel. "You want music?"

"Yeah," I said stiffly.

"You pick," he said, handing me a leather CD case.

It took a minute. I knew he could feel the thumping of the bass and the changes in tone and rhythm, but all those CDs seemed like a lot of expense to go through for that. I shook the case to get his attention. "Why?"

"They're my sister's. This is her car." He looked at me as though he thought I should know that, and put his arm on the back of my seat, turning his whole body around to look behind as he began to back out of the parking space.

I exploded into action. I didn't even know it was going to happen, but when it did, nothing could stop it. As soon as the car began to creep backward I was fighting my seatbelt, the shoulder strap, the car door. I felt like I was fighting for my life. My heart banged against my ribs in my chest and my blood thundered away from my brain to my muscles. I managed to escape the car and run about twenty feet to the bushes outside of Nacho's where I vomited. I was bent over and hurling when Shawn parked the car again and got out.

"What the hell's wrong with you?" he asked, coming after me. "What were you thinking, jumping from a moving car?" In his agitation, he was using both his voice and his hands. When I could finally look it was like watching a traffic cop.

"Sorry," I said. I was starting to shake all over and my legs got weak. I motioned him back to the car. "Sorry. You go on ahead." I started back into the bar.

"Wait," said Shawn, reaching out for me. "Are you really sick?" He turned me to face him.

One of the things about being with Shawn that had required adjustment was the fact that he often pulled me around to face him. Normally, that kind of handling wasn't a problem for me. It was an established fact that I was submissive. Not a full-on, put me in a cage, I'll eat off the floor sub, but a garden variety, doesn't mind being manhandled a little, and finds it kind of hot sub.

In the olden days I'd done more game playing. It was a bad mix with booze, and had rarely ended well. Everyone in the real scene knew that, so mostly, I would wind up with wannabes or amateurs, and it was one of the things I'd found

I didn't have a taste for without the lubrication of alcohol. But Shawn was forceful, and hot. It was a combination that, ordinarily, I welcomed. But maybe I was the kind of guy who avoided stuff by walking away, and he never let me.

I pushed his hands away. "Get your damn hands off me!" I shouted, feeling physically ill. "The hell? You think you can push me around like a damn doll?"

Shawn threw both hands in the air, as though he were being robbed. "Whoa!" he said.

I sank against the wall of the bar. Sweat trickled down my face, but I was cold and started to shiver.

"You are sick." Shawn put a hand out, indicating that I should go first into the bar.

"I can't go in there just yet." I shook my head emphatically. I was near tears or going to kill something.

"What do you want me to do?" he asked.

"Go to your play; I'll be fine. Call me at the bar tomorrow." I made that shooing motion, which was like waving a red flag at a bull.

"I'm not leaving." He was angry. "How could you think I would leave you like this?"

"I'm fine," I repeated, still shooing. I was stunned by the force of my reaction. I hadn't even tried to get into a car before because I'd ridden to rehab on my bike and never looked back.

"Look. We can go to my house and get tea."

"No," I said. I was looking at the car.

He rubbed his face with both hands, but stayed there, grim determination written in the planes of his body. My breathing was returning to a more normal, steady pace. He took off his jacket and put it around my shoulders. I had my own jacket on, but his, warm with his body heat, felt good. I was thawing. I was coming down.

"It's the car." I pointed to the parking lot. I got out my little phone and signaled that I would try to text him.

He looked back at the white Camry, then at me, got his cell phone out, and waited.

I don't ride in cars. It's a phobia, I sent. *I never tested it out. It's stronger than I thought.*

"How did you think we'd get to the play?" he asked.

My bike. I pointed to my motorcycle. His face softened a little, and he relaxed somewhat.

"You're an asshole." He let out a deep breath. "And you're going to be a lot of work, aren't you?"

Since he held on to his phone I figured he was still giving me a shot. I painstakingly typed, *I'm sorry I didn't tell you. I did a lot of spilling my guts in rehab. Exorcised a lot of demons. It wasn't a habit I wanted to cultivate or keep when I left.*

"Some things are important, if we're going out." He indicated the car.

I know. I nodded.

"Well, shit," he said, then stood for a while. "I don't feel like going to a play anymore."

I could do tea, I typed. *Or coffee.*

"Still cold?" he asked. It made me feel a funny something in my chest when he said it. I realized I was warming up from the inside.

Or hot chocolate, I typed. *But I'm getting warmer.*

It probably wasn't until that moment that I realized my development had been arrested at about fifteen, when I'd started drinking and partying with my friends, and that everything that was happening to me now was, essentially, happening to that kid. No wonder I didn't know how to do this stuff. I hadn't been in the game. I'd been lying on the sidelines, in a stupor composed of alcohol and vanity. Stupidity and ignorance and false bravado.

I am probably A LOT more work than I'm worth, I sent to his phone, by way of truth in advertising.

"I know," he said, and put his arm around me to lead me to the entrance of Nacho's.

"Alfred is here." He nodded toward the bar. "I'll ask him how he makes his spicy hot chocolate. Why don't you go clean up?" He took his jacket from around my shoulders and spoke directly into my ear. "You don't smell so good." He followed this up with a gentle kiss on my forehead and a pat on my ass. I saw him walk away, and I went to my room.

Since my shirt was wet through, I took a quick shower and changed clothes. I brushed my teeth. I was as fresh as I was going to be. When I got back downstairs, Shawn met me with a blanket, a bag, and a thermal carafe. He indicated I should follow him, and I did as he walked down the boardwalk all the way to the pier. In the darkness, the pier looked like the skeleton of some giant serpent, the hulking wooden structure slithering onto land from the sea. Its old timbers looked decrepit and splintery in this light.

I'd seen the Balboa Pier and Santa Monica Pier and knew they were tourist destinations with restaurants and fishing and bait stands. This one appeared to have no other use than simply to jut out over the water.

Shawn made his way under it, to the cool damp sand there and set out his blanket. The tide was well out. He lit a little battery-operated camping lantern and brought out chips and salsa from Nacho's, and a bowl with some of the fruit that I'd cut up for the bar. He took out cups and saucers and poured coffee, giving me creamer and sugar. He'd thought of everything, including those little sticks to stir with. He looked up at me and smiled, but it looked a little…different somehow. Sad, maybe.

I leaned over and kissed him. "Thank you."

"You're not off the hook," he said. "Tell me about cars."

I took out my phone again, waving it around until he got his. Then I typed the words I had hoped not to have to share with him. *I was in an accident*, I sent, beginning a new text message, breaking it up so I didn't have to shoot it out all at once. *I was too drunk and I gave my keys to my lover.*

Shawn frowned. "Was he killed?"

No, someone else. I couldn't close my eyes like I wanted to because I had to fucking type. I had thought about that moment maybe forty-two thousand times every day, but who's counting. *A child.*

Shawn furrowed his brow thoughtfully, but said nothing. As I watched his expressive face, I felt like I was hanging over a precipice. I picked up a piece of orange and ate it just for something to do while he made up his mind if he was going to say something. Finally, he put his hand on mine and said, "Shit, Cooper."

I remember trying to trot out some sort of a wry smile, going for resigned. "Yeah, well…"

"You still blame yourself?"

"Yes." I nodded. He had to see that I wouldn't dodge responsibility.

"I see." He sipped his coffee.

It was my fault. I gave him the keys, I texted. *It was me.*

"He could have given someone else the keys. He could have chosen not to accept them," he pointed out. "I don't understand."

"Of course you don't understand!" I threw down the phone, feeling explosive. "No one could understand unless they'd done it. No one could know what it's like unless…"

"Hey." He laid a big hand on my shoulder. "Type what you said, and then let me finish."

I pinched my lips together. "Sorry," I said. I typed as much as I could remember of my outburst.

"I don't understand why that made you afraid of cars."

My thumbs hovered over the keys. *I just can't get into one anymore. That's all.* I still couldn't talk about the chaos in the aftermath of the accident—Bobby's mother screaming, the sirens wailing. How I locked myself in the truck cab and refused to come out. Police. Firefighters and EMTs. How revolting I must have seemed at that moment, standing there, pierced and tattooed, shaking and scared sober. Worthless, yet taking up space while the world reviled me and wished me dead.

No one held me responsible; I hadn't broken any laws. It wasn't even my truck, it was his, except we shared it, and I gave him the keys that day. *I gave him the keys.* The next day, with my parents' blessing both monetary and spiritual, I took the bike to Hazelden in Center City, Minnesota, and never looked back.

Through long practice I'd learned to keep my face impassive. I used that now as I continued to drink my coffee and eat slivers of fruit that tasted like sawdust in my mouth.

"How old were you when you started drinking?" Shawn changed the subject. I was surprised, but not sorry. I began to breathe again.

"Fourteen," I replied, using my hands to show him. I had fond memories of alcohol leading to unexpected physical encounters, reducing my inhibitions, making it possible for me to step outside my rigid upbringing. Giving me an excuse for having sex with guys at a time when I still needed one. "My best friend Jordan and I started drinking around middle school. We thought we were such hot shit."

Shawn smiled. "I'm trying to imagine what fourteen-year-old Cooper was like." He popped a piece of apple into my mouth and took a maraschino cherry for himself. "I can do that trick with the stem. Watch." He held up a finger and with the other hand slowly lowered the cherry into his open mouth.

I watched and he chewed, and sure enough, the red stem came out tied. I shivered a little, remembering that tongue on my dick.

"Well?" he asked.

I had no idea what he was talking about. "Well, what?"

"What was the fourteen-year-old Cooper like?"

"I don't know." I hated stuff like this. I typed, *Maybe just an orchestra geek?*

"Nobody's 'just' an anything."

I was the first chair violin, I admitted with my thumbs, sending it in dispatches like a telegram. *I went to music camp and music lessons. I liked video games. Most of the time I was angry or horny or scared; one, both, or some exotic combination of all three.*

Shawn grinned. "You say that like it's in the past."

What? I sent. *It is in the past; he's long gone. I think I drowned him in beer.*

"Oh, I don't know." Shawn smiled. He lay on his back on the blanket, biting his lip a little as if he had a private joke. "I think I may be looking at him right now."

Chapter Seven

"It's time," said Shawn, changing the subject completely, "that you learned some sign language." All business, he sat up straight on the blanket, facing me with his legs crossed. He urged me to do likewise. "Boy," he said, pinching the air in front of his forehead. "Boy. You do it."

"Okay," I said. I felt like an utter ass, but as I was pretty sure he had worked tirelessly for years to be able to speak, I felt it incumbent on me to try signing.

"Good. Girl," he said, brushing his cheek. This went on for a while, mother, father, boy, girl, hello. I didn't see that these would be that useful for me, but I dutifully learned them and got them right when he tested me at intervals. It wasn't until he came to kiss that I began to see actual possibilities.

"Kiss," he said, gesturing to his mouth and then his cheek. I did it. "Kiss me," he signed, following "kiss" up with a finger on his chest. "Kiss me."

"Kiss me," I signed. He smiled and leaned in, catching my jaw in his hand. I wanted to keep my eyes open. Tried to. But at the last moment something overcame me and they closed. I felt his lips brush mine, the barest whisper of contact, and then I felt them smile a moment before he indicated with his tongue that he wouldn't be satisfied with just a brush. It went on and on. Gentle and undemanding. I reached for his belt buckle but he caught my hand, breaking off the kiss.

"You sign well," he said, and took the last bit of apple, biting it and sharing it with me. "Gay," he said, tapping his thumb and forefinger on his chin. "Gay, try it."

I made the sign, "Gay." I got out my phone and typed. *That looks like a beard; do you just use that for men?*

He waited patiently and looked at my text. "Yes, this is *G* and is for gay. For lesbian, you use the *L* in front of the chin, like this."

I tried it. It was going to be like learning kanji, which I'd done a bit of in high school, when I'd studied Japanese. *There's a sign for everything.* I probably even typed whiny. *How am I ever going to learn to do this?*

He gave me an exaggeratedly patient look. "You learned to play the violin. This will be hard; you have to practice. After a while, it becomes second nature."

How do you say lie down and shut the fuck up? I typed, a reasonable request, given my relationship skills.

"*You* don't." He glared at me.

"Sorry," I mumbled, looking down.

"I do," he said. He proceeded to sign, "Lie down and shut the fuck up." Or whatever its equivalent was.

"I'm sorry, I don't have that yet," I said, "Do it again slowly, so I can learn it."

"You don't need to learn it." He pushed me over onto my back. "You just need to do it." He bit me on the lower lip.

I fought him a little because I didn't want sand in those hard-to-reach places, so he and I picked up the blanket and started the walk back to Nacho's in silence. At that moment, there was nothing I wanted more than the easy companionship I'd glimpsed with him and the ability to talk to him freely in whatever language or fashion made the most sense.

I dropped the lantern and had to backtrack to pick it up. When I looked up, he was still striding away across the beach, his strong legs fighting the sucking of the sand as he moved. The breeze whipped his hair around a little; it was long, below his collar, a little wavy, and wild. As I stared at him, he realized I wasn't with him and turned back to find me. He quirked a finger at me and said, "Come on." I ran after him like an eager dog. I knew I was getting in deep here in Santo Ignacio, drowning in hope, expectation, safety, and peace. I wondered how long it would be until I realized that drowning was drowning anywhere you did it, and the end result was probably the same.

* * *

The following morning when I saw Jim I broached the subject of finding a computer to use to study sign language. Shawn wasn't there at the table—he was probably at school—but I expected he'd hear about this just the same. I took a lot of good-natured teasing.

"So, I guess we can expect you to be here for a while," said Jim, smiling. "It's the cayenne in the cocoa. It's a known aphrodisiac, of course, but it's also a powerful romantic love potion."

"I guess," I murmured, feeling a little strange.

"Nah, it's m'hijo's cooking. No one can resist a guy who cooks," said Oscar, grinning at Tomas. Everyone agreed.

"You can use the computer in the office," said Jim. "I'll set you up with your own password. Alfred does the official Nacho's Bar business work on it, but that's really all we use it for, and he's rarely here in the mornings. What are you going to look up first?" He grinned. "I can think of a few things I'd want to know how to say."

"Uh," I said, thinking this could get out of hand fast. "I just want to learn the basics. You know. Conversation."

"Oh," he said. "How disappointing." I know I was blushing, thinking about the previous night and wondering whether the first thing I'd do would be to establish a signed safe word.

"Well, thank you," I said, probably a little stiffly. "You just let me know when it's free and I'll use it then." I finished my breakfast and went to the kitchen.

There's a certain geographical area of safety around prepping onions. There were other kitchen helpers, three busboys besides Shawn, and four waiters. For various reasons, I hadn't made friends with them yet. We'd exchanged tentative smiles and nodded at one another, but the other kitchen guys spoke only broken English, and my second language, sketchy as it was, was Japanese.

I was aware that I'd landed in Santo Ignacio behind all kinds of language barriers. I was beginning to learn a little Spanish, and the guys were warming up to me. None of them were gay, and they had mixed feelings about me, I could tell, and about Oscar and Tomas, who were ambiguous in a teasing way but still completely undemonstrative.

On the one hand, Nacho's was definitely a gay bar, and mostly patronized by men at night. Yet on the other hand, because of Shawn, it seemed to be where the local deaf kids hung out, regardless of gender, and it had the number one family brunch and drew people from all over. Because of that sometimes it felt like purgatory, like we were all at some kind of way station, a place for nourishing the spirit and reflecting until we were ready to move on. The lifers, as I liked to call Jim and Alfred, never moved on at all.

Shawn showed up at five or so, and as he was throwing on his work apron I hit him with my new skill, asking him in sign language, "How was your day?" This had taken me most of the morning to perfect.

He stared at me for a while with something nice in his eyes. "Fine, how was yours?" Well. Shit. I had nothing. He grinned and pulled me into the employee bathroom to kiss me.

"Hey," I said.

"Your hands smell like onions and garlic," he said, holding one up to his nose. He pushed me against the door.

"I've been prepping veg," I said. I made the sign for kiss me, and he did. I felt for his belt buckle, and he caught my hand.

"No," he said. He sucked up a mark on my neck, under my tattoo. I could feel the heat from his mouth, his breath. It was becoming a habit with him, starting things and not following through.

"What the hell?" I spoke into his mouth.

"What?" he asked, perplexed.

I gestured to his hands and his buckle.

"I'm working; so are you." He stared at me. "I just wanted a kiss."

"Oh," I said, feeling stupid.

"I could fuck you every time we kiss, but I'd have to kiss you less."

"Or fuck me more." I grinned. I think he read my lips, based on the sparkle in his eyes.

"Later, it's a promise." He left the bathroom and I waited a few minutes until I had myself under better control. I looked in the mirror and I didn't recognize myself for a second. Of course, regular sleep and showers made a difference, but I thought I looked altered somehow in other ways. My eyes were the same green as always but there was less tightness about them. I wasn't holding my jaw as though any minute someone would break it. I felt like my shoulders were looser, and my breathing was deeper and more relaxed. Maybe more oxygen was getting to my brain. I looked…younger.

I left the bathroom feeling a spring in my step I hadn't felt in a long time.

"Hey, m'hijo," said Oscar. "My sister gave me a box of mangoes from the club store. You want one?"

"Yeah," I said, catching it when he tossed it to me. I cut it up and flipped it inside out before slicing off the cubes. I was eating it when Shawn came back into the kitchen with a tub full of dirty dishes. As though it were the most natural thing in the world, he leaned over and I fed him some mango bits off my fork. His hand came up and he played with my hair, pushing it back behind my ear. We shared a sticky mango kiss, and he moved on. Oscar and Tomas were staring at me.

"That was the cutest thing I think I've ever seen, bro," Oscar teased. I ducked my head and turned to wash my hands and get back to work. "I take it back," he said to Tomas. "Nobody can resist a guy who cooks *and* plays the violin."

Tomas laughed at my discomfort. "What's wrong, Cooper?" he asked. "It's not like you've never had a boyfriend before." He went back to work, arguing with Oscar as they prepared food and plated orders.

I had a boyfriend?

I had a boyfriend. Had I ever had one before? I'd had lovers. Lots of them. I looked at Shawn carefully the next few times he moved in and out of the kitchen. If I did have a boyfriend and Shawn was it, I was a damned lucky son of a bitch. He was gorgeous, nice, funny, and frightening in the sack, in a good way. He made me feel things, in and out of bed, that I'd never felt before. Stupid things. Naive things. Things I didn't believe and couldn't put my trust in. That and I wanted to hump his leg like a dog every time I saw him. *Shit.*

When it came time for me to play and Jim turned off the overhead music, I took the opportunity to lose myself. I think I played the best I'd ever played that night, relaxed and happy in the cozy waterfront bar. Patrons clapped and some even pushed a couple of empty tables back and danced, as I switched from mariachi to Irish music. I fiddled my way through some standard pub fare and even played a couple of love ballads, which several couples danced to romantically, touching and kissing around the restaurant. I saw Shawn smiling at me, looking at me in a way no one had ever looked at me, and I felt full to bursting with something I couldn't name.

Later, Shawn took me upstairs. He had this habit of catching my hand and pulling me along like a duck on a string, which I hate to say I found endearing. I knew he was younger than me by six years at twenty-two, and he was still in school and bused tables at a bar for money. I didn't know much of anything about his family, or his home life, or even what he studied in school. He knew less than that, I'm sure, about me. But when he pulled me to his body that night, he played me like I played the violin, and all the notes were perfect and clear and sweet. He gave me pleasure like I'd never known and pulled from me a kind of surrender that I'd never dared to experience. I gave him complete control, and he could have cut off my air and I would have kept my eyes on his in absolute willing submission and died.

I loved him. *I loved him.*

"Hey," he said, interlacing his fingers with mine and pulling a sheet up over our sweating bodies. He faced me on the narrow bed, no mean feat, his nose only inches from mine. I could smell beer on his breath, and I'm sure he could smell cigarettes on mine. I felt a half smile creep over me; *goofy*, I thought.

He put a finger on the corner of my mouth. "Tell me something without words…"

I began to pull him closer to me to kiss him, maybe go for round two. He held me back.

"Without words or sex." He smiled.

I thought, *Shit, what did I have to tell him?* My ASL coup of the day, "How was your day?" was useless to me now. I rolled my eyes.

"Good. That tells me I make you crazy," he teased.

I tried to think of something that wasn't too stupid. Finally, I lifted his hand and kissed it, then placed it over my heart so he could feel it beating.

"Oh," he said. "*Oh.* I like how you think. Mmph..." He buried his face in my shoulder. "Now, shut the fuck up already so we can get some sleep."

I remember putting an arm around him, thinking I'd never been so content. He snored. I was good with that, except after a while I thought maybe the wrong one of us was deaf.

Chapter Eight

As usual, Sunday brunch at Nacho's started out under a thick blanket of fog. By two o'clock, though, it burned off, leaving the palest blue sky with just a dusting of clouds. Not much of a wind blew, and what there was seemed crisp and clean. Shawn and I got to leave work early, a special treat, and we headed out on my bike for a ride. I could tell that Shawn had never ridden a motorcycle, so we took it slow. I let him get the feel of the Sportster as we wound our way along Pacific Coast Highway between the beach communities there, until we would get to a town and traffic would crawl, all the other tourists out doing the same thing.

Something settled inside me then, a deep serenity, the kind I thought I would get from rehab, but didn't. It wasn't Shawn. He was part of the picture, but I knew better than to expect someone to fill my empty spaces. I thought it might have been the act of standing in one place long enough to look around. I was taking stock in St. Nacho's, making a new list of what I didn't want and, maybe more importantly, what I did

I liked laughing, I found out, and music. I liked nice people, getting up early, and working hard. I liked simple pleasures, like my toes in the sand and someone to kiss. I didn't have to understand Heisenberg's uncertainty principle, or why Mahler stayed only one year with the Metropolitan Opera. I just had to chop onions into neat little pieces. I could stop in St. Nacho's and do what I'd been doing, and though I had a definite preference, I could be happy with or without Shawn. Shawn's presence at my back on that ride was a bonus.

We stopped at a restaurant in Morro Bay called The Galley and ate Dungeness crab cocktails. Shawn tried opakapaka because he liked the name, and I had albacore with grilled vegetables. Time slowed down with Shawn, each moment stretching longer as I watched him. One of the things he began to do was teach me the sign for every single item we came in contact with. I thought my head would explode, but the pleasure he displayed when I got it right made me continue on with the game, and it was a game because he made it fun all through the day.

"Fish," he said and signed. His hand moved like a fish through the water. "Fish."

"Fish," I signed.

We did table, napkin, knife, fork, spoon, plate, glass, bread, water, ice. He asked me which words I remembered. I went blank. "Fish," I signed.

Shawn rubbed his face. "Good," he said finally.

I'll take a class, I texted him. *I found one online. I gave Jim the money.* Shawn's smile was like the sun.

"Thank you," he said, sticking out his tongue in a vulgar way.

"You're welcome," I said, and signed a nasty little message of my own.

Watching him eat, I noticed his every movement. How he sipped his beer, how he used his utensils, the drops of condensation from his water goblet that wet his lips and he licked off, unaware that I was looking. In an agony of self-conscious discomfort, I slowed my usual quick pace to his more leisurely one, wanting to do everything just right.

This kind of thing had been much easier with the addition of alcohol to ease the tension. I was covered in a kind of social rust, made worse by my age and his expectations.

Oil me.

Shawn took the check and wouldn't give it up when I attempted to pay. He both spoke and gestured that it was his treat and ended up leaving cash and a generous tip. He threw an arm around me as we walked out of the restaurant. People stared at us, some in frank disapproval. I was exploding with pride. I'd never felt such numbing gratitude. I drove us back to St. Nacho's, hyperaware of him behind me. His warm hands slipped around me and he leaned forward. Sometimes I felt him press against me in a deliberate hug.

We returned to the bar, which was empty and dark, and walked up the stairs together. I felt all new, somehow, and different in a way I couldn't explain but it made me hesitant. It was as if anything I did from that point on counted. Shawn turned the knob and opened the door, and I walked in ahead of him. He leaned back against it once he closed it. Things stood still for a minute. Time hung on me like old clothes, dragging me down. I started to take off my leather jacket because suddenly I didn't want to be wearing it. It marked me as the property of some other man, now almost forgotten in the haze of distant memory. My recollection was faulty anyway and filled with gaps and holes like overproofed bread. I dropped the jacket and kicked it to the corner of the small room.

"Hey, you," said Shawn, looking relaxed. I saw him swallow hard and it made me smile.

"Hey." I stood where I was, preferring to let him take the lead. If in conversational situations I felt rusty, in this I was wholly new.

He gestured to me. "Come here."

I went. Beginning at the top of my head, he used his hands to graze lightly over me, like he would have petted an animal, letting his touch soothe and introduce us all over again.

"Pretty," he said, and I laughed. He fingered my ear where I was pierced all the way from lobe to cartilage and the eyebrow where I had the tiny barbell. His lips rose in a smile, really just on one side. It was monstrous how much I wanted him. He thumbed near my eyes and then over my eyelids as they closed. He tipped my head back and his lips came down on mine, tentatively at first, but inquiring, as if he were asking for entrance. I slid my hands around his back and down to his ass, content to just rest them there. He opened my mouth and his tongue crept in as he cupped and cradled my face.

I responded with enthusiasm, kissing, tasting, and touching him, going as slow as I had at the meal, wanting to experience every second fully. But like blood moving to a frozen extremity, my return to human interaction wasn't without discomfort. I felt unbearably awkward, relying heavily on him to show me what he liked, to tell me what to do to please him. I knew I wanted to go from being passive to actively pleasing him, to giving instead of just taking. I had a moment of real respect for the ease of being thrown against a wall and fucked hard. It made me smile.

"What?" asked Shawn.

"It's nothing." I shook my head and slipped a hand under his jacket to help him ease it off. He closed his eyes. I threw his jacket to the floor with mine, and it hit the scarred wooden floor with a thud. Then I went after his T-shirt. Once I had it off, I admired the hard planes of his chest and belly, the strength in his arms. I didn't know what he did for exercise, only that it worked. I guessed he danced. Maybe did track in school. He was long, lean, and rangy. Strong, but not bulky. He wrapped his hands around my neck, kneading my shoulders.

"Are you tense?" he asked.

"No," I replied, looking down. "Yes." I nodded. We stood there for a few minutes, kissing like teenagers. He kissed with his whole body, and I responded with mine. *Bliss.*

He walked me toward my small bed and seated me on it, then toed off his shoes and socks before removing his jeans. He slid out of his shorts and stood before me, erect, handsome, and silent.

"What can I do?" I asked him, struggling out of my own jeans.

"What?" he asked.

I leaned down and untied my boots and tossed them out of the way, along with my socks. I made sure he could see my lips. "What can I do for you?" I asked again. I tried to make him understand by speaking very crisply, but I felt like an idiot. "What do you like?" I held my breath, unaccountably shy.

"I like *you*," he said, lying down next to me, not touching but close, facing me. I dug a pillow from behind me and offered it to him. He put it under his head. "I like *you*, Cooper."

I touched his face as I'd wanted to the first time I saw it, exploring it with my fingertips. I let my hands play over its contours and thumbed his lips. "So pretty," I muttered.

"What?" he asked, lifting my face.

"Pretty," I said. "Beautiful." I had learned "you" in ASL. "You," I demonstrated. "Beautiful."

He smiled. "*Beautiful.*" He showed me how to make the word, a finger, surrounding his face. I did it.

Teasing, he grabbed my hand. "Stop talking," he said, and pulled me to him.

I just entwined myself around him and let him do what he wanted. He touched me all over, breathed me in and licked me. He was everywhere at once. His tongue was on some sort of quest to find deeper and more hidden places, the more ticklish the better. We rolled and nuzzled, rubbed and groaned, until I felt frenzied and he was covered in a sheen of salty sweat.

"Here," he said, pulling me down on top of him and lifting his legs. I probably looked at him like I'd never seen him before.

"What?" I asked. *Oh, I knew what.* I was stalling for time.

"My ass is what," he said impatiently. "Fuck me?" His open face held nothing that looked like a challenge in it.

"Oh, hey…"

"Don't you?" he asked, relaxing his legs back down. "Really, don't you like it?"

"I don't dislike it," I said, hedging, aware that he didn't understand because I'd mumbled.

"You don't want me like that?" He looked into my eyes.

I couldn't help the look that passed over my face. I was sure it told him everything he needed to know.

"You're scared," he said.

I shook my head.

"It's all right. You don't have to."

"I want to," I said, lowering my eyes. I made damn sure he could read my lips. "I *really* want to."

His face relaxed into an easy grin. "Come here," he said on a sigh. "We'll go slow, all right?" Oh. *Slow.*

I found the lube and upended it in my hand, squirting a small amount onto my fingertips. I wanted to warm it, so I rubbed it back and forth between them, and then looked at my fingers again, wondering if I still had enough. It didn't matter that Shawn wanted this. I was going to second-guess my way through the entire thing. Shawn tugged on my shoulder and I looked up. He appeared to be laughing at me.

I slid down so I could see what I was doing, and I think he sucked in air and bit his lip when I touched his dick with my tongue. It came alive in my mouth, and I nuzzled his balls on my way down, finding the smooth strip of skin behind them and nibbling on that. I tongued his hole and breached it, savoring the soft keening sounds I heard him make.

There were times when his unmusical voice was like a symphony to me.

I used a finger to stroke the tightly puckered flesh, dark in the dim light. I found myself clenching my teeth as I entered him with it, holding my breath until he gave way and his tight muscles let me in. I didn't have to ask. This wasn't his usual thing either. We were forging new bonds here, charting new territory that would be only ours, and I felt it in his indrawn breath whenever my finger moved.

"Baby," he moaned, his hand stroking my hair as I watched my fingers claim his hole. "Oh, good." He shifted his hips, riding my hand, and I added another finger.

Since I knew he couldn't hear me, I contented myself with kissing the hollow of his abdomen, a sensitive place for him, and murmuring words there, so he knew I was talking. "Sweet," I said, licking and blowing the skin in that sensitive place so he felt the cool, wet kiss. His own cock was leaving a trail on his hip that I lapped up, tasting the salty, sticky fluid. It was so erotic, so bittersweet in my mouth it made my own cock leak onto his leg. I added a third finger, and he seemed stretched and full. His hips came off the bed when I touched his spongy prostate gland, and I brushed it again, feeling him jerk against me.

"Oh, yes!" he said, catching my hair and trying to pull me up. "*Shit*, Cooper."

I slid up to face him, taking one of the condoms that he'd brought from the pillow next to his head. I couldn't help kissing him. I wanted the moment to last forever. I wanted to crawl inside him. I rolled the condom onto my cock and nudged at his entrance, silently asking permission.

"Shawn?" I asked, when I realized he was waiting for me to look at him.

"Cooper." He smiled. He interlaced his fingers with mine. "Nobody but you, Cooper."

I froze. "What?" I asked.

"It's not my style," he said. "But I don't want anything between us, nothing unfinished, you understand?" he asked me, not just with his words but with his eyes and his heart.

I nodded. "Shawn?"

"Go, baby," he said, and I did. Heaven help me, I surged into that sweet ass and stayed, as if glued inside him. "Oh, fuck, Cooper," he said, clutching my hip with his free hand.

I remained motionless as his muscles eased around me. He winced at the fullness, and I wondered how he was handling the burn I'd no doubt caused in my impatience. A drop of sweat rolled off my nose and landed almost in his eye and he laughed. I could feel the sound of his laughter all the way to my heart.

"Move," he said, taking a deep breath. He grinned suddenly and said in that awkward voice of his, "Drive it like you stole it, Cooper."

I dropped my head to his to kiss those luscious lips and let myself go.

By the time our hips were snapping together and I felt that chill in my spine, he was pushing off the tiny headboard with both hands and I had his legs on my shoulders to drive my cock into his ass as hard as he wanted it. I fisted his cock, pumping it and running my thumb over the slit on its head until it rocketed in my hands and his entire body clenched around me. I pumped into him once, twice, and filled the condom on the third stroke as we gasped and shuddered and came down together.

Shawn put both arms around me to embrace me as his legs slid down, and I slipped out a few minutes later and pulled off the condom to throw it into the trash. I let him gather me close and clung to him. I don't know how long we stayed that way. I knew I would never move again if I had any choice in the matter. He spoke to me in nonsense words as he drifted, and I hummed into his skin. I knew he felt it because he began to rock in time, just fractionally, moving his body to my little tune. I think it was "The Polonaise."

"You make music all the time." He sighed.

I nodded.

"What fucking irony."

I expelled a breath of laughter and nodded again. I could feel him smile against my skin.

"It will make a good story later on." I could tell he was drifting away; he always fell asleep first.

"What?" I tapped his face and when his eyes opened, I asked, "What story?"

"Our story. Yours and mine."

That made me smile. It was the first time since I'd held a Hot Wheels in my hands that I showed my naked pleasure to another guy.

Chapter Nine

I could hear the kitchen starting up and smell the beginnings of breakfast cooking. Oscar must have been in, sautéing onions and celery, and probably had stock simmering. I was in Jim and Albert's office, signing my way through foods: pizza, spaghetti, and tacos. I wasn't registered in my class yet so I was working from the ASL Browser, learning what I could from the list of words there. It seemed impossible to me. I tried not to think about how many words there were; I just concentrated on one at a time. I also took the opportunity to send e-mails to my family, who appeared to be relieved I was alive.

I wanted to send something to my sister Julie especially. Julie answered immediately with big virtual hugs and a picture of her little coffeehouse, Hallowed Grounds. We'd exchanged infrequent e-mails in the past, mostly from library computers, or when I'd borrow a little cyber time from hook-ups. I usually dashed off very brief or even instant messages. She seemed relieved to know where she could reach me. I even gave her the phone number of the bar in case she needed me or had news about our folks that couldn't wait.

I tried to explain Santo Ignacio, but there were no words. I only said that I had found a job and a place to stay, and that I was happy. Julie would understand.

Julie had been the one to hold me when I'd puked and cried. Julie had attended the family counseling sessions at Hazelden in my parents' stead. Julie had been there when I got out of rehab, waiting with balloons and flowers, and had returned home shocked and alone when I'd gotten on my Harley and roared off toward the Pacific. Seven million and fucking *one* amends to make.

Thinking, I sat with my eyes closed for a minute, and before I opened them, a pair of strong hands found the knots that were building in my shoulders, between the blades.

I reached back and found Shawn's face and pulled him in for a kiss. He didn't speak. I pressed my cheek against his newly shaven one and held it there. He smelled like limes, I guess from his shaving cream, and I wanted to start something. He brushed against me and left. I knew he had classes and Kevin was probably waiting outside. I logged off the computer and went to help in the kitchen.

"Oh, hey, m'hijo," said Oscar. "Let me make you a cup of coffee with a little foam heart on the top."

Tomas grinned and joined in. "I thought maybe we should just peel him some grapes, papi," he teased. "Shawn looked pretty happy when he left just now."

"I *make* him happy," I said, gathering a big bowl of garlic to peel and chop. "'Cause I'm all that and a bag of chips." I waved the chef's knife around a little.

"Yeah, m'hijo, buffalo chips."

"Are you talking to me?" I asked.

"Watch it, papi," said Tomas. "Boy's got a knife."

"I can see we're having fun this morning," said Jim, who went to get himself some coffee. "Are we waving knives around this early? Must be spring. So, how's our tattooed love god? Shawn left you a message." He grinned, and I got a bad feeling about it.

"What?" I asked, and all three of them leaped on me, knife forgotten, and kissed my face.

"Jeez!" I said. "Watch it; somebody's going to be a eunuch, man." I laughed but felt my face burn.

"Holy crap," said Jim, staring. "If I hadn't seen it for myself, I wouldn't have believed it."

"What?" I started on the garlic, figuring the peppers would wait and I'd have to use gloves with them anyway, which I hate.

"You laughed. And blushed." He took a chip that Oscar pulled from the fryer and waved it around, blowing on it. "Santo Ignacio, man, it's in the water." He left the kitchen.

"What's that supposed to mean?" I asked Tomas, who shrugged and dumped the tortilla chips into the chilaquile sauce.

Oscar was breaking eggs to scramble them. "He means that Santo Ignacio? It's the kind of place a man can drop his shit. It's a place for healing, m'hijo. And you looked like you could use it, back when you came."

"Yeah," I said, mincing the garlic and catching it up with the knife for him to use with the eggs. "I guess I needed a place like this." I felt an unfamiliar sensation in the muscles of my face and realized it was a goofy grin.

"Stop that smiling, bro—you're creeping me out. Man smiles like that... He's getting some."

"Oh, hell yeah." I laughed. I kept cutting garlic into small, even pieces. What I had with Shawn was coloring the rest of my life like a red T-shirt in the laundry with white socks. I didn't have a thing to compare it to in my experience. Thinking about him made me smile, no matter what I was doing or where I was doing it. No matter that he wasn't with me. When I thought of Shawn, a well of *something* boiled up inside me that hit my heart like an air bubble and stopped it, metaphorically speaking, making me feel dazed. All I could think was, *What the hell is that all about?*

By the time I started playing for the tables that evening, I was pleasantly tired. I wove between the customers playing requests, and much to Jim's dismay they were mostly for the Irish fiddling tunes I'd begun to introduce a few nights before.

I heard him shout, "You're turning my cantina into a pub, gringo," but I shrugged it off. I played what the customers asked for, and he knew it. Someone was having an anniversary party, and they had a lovely cake. Grinning, I played "Hava Nagila" at their request and turned to find Jim shaking his head. Shawn came in with some of his friends and acknowledged me with a jerk of his head and a smile. I noticed Kevin was absent from their group. At about seven I was playing "De Colores" when Jim motioned me to the bar.

I finished up and walked over. He told me there was someone on the phone for me.

I took the phone, plugging my ear with a finger so I could hear over the crowd. "Hello?"

"Cooper?" asked a male voice. He cleared his throat and said my name again. "Cooper? Is that you?"

"Jordan?" My heart slammed against my rib cage.

"Yeah." He chuckled. "You still know my voice."

I said nothing; shock made my blood drain to my toes.

"Hey… Julie gave me this number; she said you were staying in some bar in California?"

"Yeah." Right then there was an explosion of sound from the anniversary party as someone gave a comic toast.

Jim's concerned eyes were on me. "You can take that in the office, line one." He pointed to the phone on the wall. "It's quieter." He had to shout to make himself heard.

I nodded. "Jordan," I said. "Don't hang up, I'm going someplace quieter. Okay?"

"Yeah," he said. I gave the phone back to Jim.

As I walked to the office, a thousand things went through my head. I sat in Alfred's chair and stared at the phone for a full minute before I leaned toward it. I knew my past. I knew my heart. I picked up the phone with a shaking hand. "Jordan," I said.

"Cooper, it's good to hear your voice."

"Yours too…" I fumbled. "Are you out?"

"Out? Yeah, I got out about a month ago." The silence between us was thick and ugly. "You never visited."

"No," I said. "I didn't. I didn't stick around."

"I know. You went to Minnesota and then out west. I got the postcards," he said.

"My parents…"

"I know. They wanted you gone." There was a long pause on the line. "I got it. I was sorry not to see you, but I understood. Julie told me."

Julie. Still cleaning up my messes. "Jules is a brick," I said, not feeling the love at that particular moment.

"Yeah." I knew he was squeezing the phone, I could feel the pressure he was putting on it from my side. "Listen. I…I wonder if you'd think about coming back."

"No, I don't think so." *No.*

"Things have changed though, now. You know? I've changed. I went through stuff, man. Stuff I can't even tell you, and you know I love you. I need you."

"Jordie," I said, automatically going back to the old name, the old ways… *No.*

"Coop, I'm sober now. I go to this church, babe. You'd laugh so hard, but they're good people. They don't care if you're gay or straight; they say we're all who we're supposed to be if we just follow…"

"Jordie—" I began again, but he cut me off.

"No!" he said, and I could hear the old desperation in his voice. "No, just hear me out, Coop. I got that you didn't get in trouble, and I was glad! We didn't both need to go to jail. But, man, I'm out and I need you. You said you loved me. You said we were partners. I've done everything for both of us for the last three years. I took it for the team. I need you."

I swallowed hard and closed my eyes. They burned. "What do you need, Jordie?"

"I need help. I'm sober, but I'm scared. I'm staying at Mom's now but I'm moving out soon, and I'll be all by myself. Nobody's going to want to hire me, an ex-con who killed a kid... I'm afraid. Nobody gets it but you. I need you with me. I need my partner back. You're sober, right? You're clean?"

"Yeah, I'm clean." Except cigarettes, I was so fucking clean I squeaked.

"I need you to help me stay sober. I need someone to be there for me. I know why you couldn't be there when I was in jail. But now it's different, right? Now we can live like we always thought we were going to. But better, right?"

I couldn't answer him.

"Cooper?" He reached out to me with his voice. "I think you owe me at least this... I think we owe ourselves, and we for damned sure owe that kid. I want to try to be something better. Please say you'll help me."

"Yeah," I said, finally accepting the inevitable. "Yeah, okay. I'll be in touch." He said something, maybe a lot of stuff, and hung up. I held on to the phone for a while, listening to it make that awkward electronic hum when the connection is broken, then begin a recorded message because I didn't hang it up quickly enough. I was taking stock, hands and feet cold, brain numb, stomach faintly sick, when Shawn came to find me. Since I had my head in my hands, he probably had a clue to my mood.

"Hey, Cooper?" he asked, as he entered. He turned the office chair around and he bent so we were at the same level.

"Jim said you were in here. You got a phone call... Bad news?"

I turned to him. "I'm going home," I said.

"What?" he asked. "*What?*"

I didn't have my phone, so I searched around for a piece of paper. "I'm going home," I wrote.

"When?" He looked at the paper, not at me.

I took it out of his hands and wrote, "Now. Soon. As soon as possible I guess." I looked at the ground between where he was squatting back on the heels of his Vans and my feet.

"Okay," he said. "For how long?"

"I don't know." I lifted my shoulders. I couldn't stand the look in his eyes. It said he was secure, disappointed, but not yet aware of his mistaken assumption that I would be coming back. *That he would want me back.* What I was thinking must have shown on my face.

"What?" he asked.

"I'm not coming back," I wrote. The minute I wrote it I regretted it. Not because it hurt him, but because it closed off that tenuous place between us, where we'd agreed tacitly to try to communicate. If he didn't give me his eyes, if I didn't enunciate my words, if he didn't read what I wrote or look at his phone, all communication would prove impossible.

"Never?" he asked, only half looking at me. Should I just nod, or shake my head? Had we come to that?

I reached for his hand.

"Explain," he said, gripping my hand so hard it brought tears to my eyes. I grabbed another piece of paper. On it, I wrote the tersest account of the accident, its aftermath, and the responsibility I bore. I told him I had to go to support my friend, who'd paid the price for both of us. I told him I didn't have a choice. I told him I had to see Jordan through this. I told him I had to go pack. I watched him grind his teeth in silence.

"Go," he said. "Pack." He looked tired. "I'll be up when I get off work." He turned his back and walked away.

My gear was stowed when Shawn finally came upstairs. He didn't look at it, but rather pressed his lips firmly together and came to me. He pulled me toward him in a crushing hug, which I returned, imbuing it with everything I was feeling. I started to speak.

"Don't say anything," he commanded me, taking my face between his hands. "No words, okay?"

I nodded. He made love to me then with a desperation I felt through my skin to my bones. I know I strained against him, hoping I could just melt into him. I pulled his hair and bit his skin. I wanted to devour him. He didn't hold back a thing, and when he shuddered to a climax in my arms I thought I'd never see anything more beautiful than that for the rest of my life. I prepared myself for that. He touched something deep inside me. I didn't want anyone, ever, to touch me that way again.

* * *

I swallowed the burning in my throat when I said good-bye at breakfast the next day. Jim smiled a bittersweet smile and assured me that I'd always have a place in Santo Ignacio.

I shook my head as though it were a joke. Oscar and Tomas looked at me, concerned, and made lame jokes about cutting up their own onions again, until they could find some other stupid gringo to do it for them. Shawn followed me to my bike.

Neither of us spoke for a long time. He pulled my hand out of my jacket pocket and put something in it. *The cell phone.*

"I can't take this," I said.

"Take it. Text me," he said. "You could keep in touch. Send me text messages so I'd know…"

"I can't take this. You know that." I was shaking my head as he caught it between his hands. I hated the way hope died in his eyes. "I can't," I said.

He took his phone back. "This is really good-bye?"

I nodded.

He pulled me to him and pressed his cheek to mine. "No," he whispered. "It doesn't have to be."

I said nothing. What could I say?

"You don't have to go to him," he spat, holding my face so we were eye to eye. "There for *him*, so he can make you feel responsible, when you did nothing!"

"You don't know!" I said, wondering if it made any sense to talk without a phone or at least a paper and pencil.

"You handed your keys over. You knew better."

"Once," I said, holding up my finger. I shook my head. I knew he'd never understand why I was leaving. The one time something bad had happened Jordan was behind the wheel, but there had been hundreds of other times it could have happened when I'd been driving.

"Go," he said.

Was it wrong of me to want to kiss him? I put on my helmet. I got on the bike and kick-started it. It roared to life. I knew even though Shawn couldn't hear the roar of my Harley, he could feel it in the empty spaces of his body.

I began to ease away, out of the alley by the boardwalk where I parked my bike behind Nacho's, onto PCH. Hardly a soul was driving there this time of day, as dawn still glowed a little bluish through the marine layer. I looked in my rearview mirror and saw Shawn tearing down the street after me, chasing my bike, chasing me, his arms pistoning, his long legs pumping as he followed at a dead run.

I stopped on the side of the road and had my helmet off in seconds. "What?" I shouted as he ran up, as if he could hear me. "What is it?"

"Kiss me," he cried, throwing himself into my arms. "Kiss me, kiss me," he murmured against my skin, as he held me that last time. He kissed me deeply, pulling me to him as if to draw strength from the embrace. A car went by, honking its horn, startling both of us. I looked into his amber-colored eyes and discovered desolation and wet lashes. They told me everything I wanted to know, and maybe much, much more. Finally, he ended the kiss, giving a last lick to my lower lip.

"'Bye," he said again, and stood to watch me ride away.

I raised my gloved hand and took off again, and this time, I didn't look back.

Chapter Ten

We sat in a semicircle of battered metal folding chairs, each of us armed with the New International Version Study Bible. Mine had been a gift from Jordie, lovingly inscribed with a message and the date, given to me when I first returned to River Falls. That first week was a blur. Well-meaning friends and relatives came to welcome me home. My parents were distant but nice. Julie held an impromptu get-together with people I hadn't seen since high school at her upscale coffee place on Main Street. They were a loud bunch, and each of them questioned me at length about why I no longer drank, indicating that this seemingly Herculean task was somehow the defining change of my life. More than one pitying glance shot my way.

To be fair, I must have looked miserable. I missed Shawn and Santo Ignacio with a kind of ever-present dull ache that probably showed itself on my face like a migraine. There were times, I admit, when I found it unbearable.

"Coop?" Jordie was talking to me, and I was off somewhere else.

"Oh, hey. What?" I asked him. They were looking over Paul's letter to the Corinthians, something I remembered from Sunday school and the many weddings I'd been to where "The greatest of these is love" was improperly imported and tattooed onto cocktail napkins.

"What do you think that means?" asked our Bible study leader, Jordan's pastor, Stan. "Was he talking about romantic love?"

I looked at him to gauge whether he was kidding. One glance told me he was dead earnest. "I…um…always thought they were talking about unselfish love, like taking care of your neighbors and seeing to their needs."

"Right." He smiled a toothy smile. "Right. Paul is talking here about the second great commandment. Do you know what that is?" he asked the group.

Jordie raised his hand like a kid. Like, oh, oh, pick me, *pick me*. "It's 'love thy neighbor as thyself.'" He seemed genuinely pleased.

"That's right, Jordan. Thank you," said Stan. I looked around again. There were eight of us crammed into the small den in Stan's house, which smelled like cats. Not bad, really, not that heinous litter-box smell, but just the kind of smell you associate with cats. Stan lived with his aging mother, who had four small-boned cats to whom she'd given alphabetical names, Abner, BartholeMew, CharleMange, and DewDrop. That I knew the names of her cats didn't surprise me anymore.

"May I go outside and smoke?" I asked suddenly, startling Stan, and I guess, everyone who was intent on whatever he was saying.

"Yes." Stan smiled. "But for your body's sake, I'd like to see you quit." It was as if he'd made a motion in a student council meeting because two of the women there said, "hear, hear." I half expected someone to say motion carried.

I smiled my barest smile, one I pulled out for times when I had no other. "I should, shouldn't I?"

I left the room to a chorus of agreement. Stan's backyard was lovely. His mother was a gardening enthusiast, and at this time of year it showed up in flowers long since blooming in California. She even had poppies, which I love, and the last of her tulips. I sat on a small wrought iron bench and smoked. After a few minutes of quiet, Jordie joined me.

"Hey," he said, lighting his own cigarette off mine. "Everyone in rehab smoked."

"I remember. We lived on cigarettes, coffee, and angst."

"What was it like? At Hazelden."

"I don't remember," I lied. "I was messed up."

"Ah." He took a drag and looked thoughtfully at a small birdhouse Stan's mother kept filled with sunflower seeds. Squirrels probably ate most of them. "I know this isn't your kind of thing." He indicated our clothing, dress trousers, crisp white shirts, ties. We looked like missionaries. "I just... I like to fill the time with stuff that's healthy, you know? People like Stan are good for me to hang out with. He doesn't see us as bad."

"That's good then," I said gently.

"In that Nacho's place," he began. "You had somebody there, didn't you?"

"Yes," I said. I got up and looked around for an ashtray, and found one next to the door on the cement patio floor. I picked it up and brought it back to the bench, then set it between us. "That's over. I left it when I came back here. It wouldn't be right."

"I see."

"Did you have anyone? I mean, you know, where you were?"

"In prison?" He looked at me and laughed. "I don't *remember.*" He used my words about rehab back to me, and I realized he hadn't been fooled. "It's better that way, don't you think?"

"Yeah," I said. "I hope you know that I'm here to help in any way I can, I don't know what you expect from me. I'm trying to figure out what I'm doing here and how I can support you, but I can't just…start where we left off."

"Coop? You're wearing a tie today because I asked you to. We're way past where we left off." I felt my shoulders drop a little, like maybe some of the tension had left my body, but my head still hurt. "You know I don't expect more than you can give me, right?"

"I…" I fought for the words. "It's going to take me some time to get used to all this."

He nodded. "Stan doesn't like it when I smoke." He blew out a thick stream.

"Well," I said. "You're bound to piss some people off no matter what you do, you know?"

He punched my arm, grinning. "That's comforting." He stubbed his cigarette out and went back inside. I rubbed my arm. That was going to leave a mark.

* * *

The last of our meager moving boxes finally came up the two flights of stairs to our apartment. I went to the kitchen to order pizza for the people from church who had helped us move in. I think I had maybe four boxes altogether, and that included things I brought from my parents' house. It amazed me that my life amounted to little more than that. Jordie was feeling gregarious, I noticed, and was holding court. He used to do that when we were kids, his big, lanky body perfect for throwing an arm around you and dragging you into whatever he had going. He was currently telling the men and women who helped us that it was a shame he couldn't offer them beer for their troubles.

"That's all right," said Stan. "You get us some pizza and we'll all call it even, won't we?"

Everyone agreed enthusiastically.

"Pizza's on its way," I said, coming in from where I'd phoned in the kitchen. It was nice having a group of friends there. I was certain when they all went home they'd leave behind an awkward silence. Our apartment had only one bedroom and one bed. It was Jordan's. I planned to sleep on the couch in the living room, graciously donated by Jordan's parents, and we'd share the bathroom. The apartment wasn't too bad, actually. It was much nicer than my studio in St. Nacho's. It had big windows, a view of the small park across the street, and a tiny balcony where I could smoke until the weather got too bad.

Stan came over to me while Jordan supervised putting the boxes into the correct rooms. "I'm glad to get a chance to talk to you," he said, holding out his hand. I took it, and we shook firmly. "This is good, this place."

"Yeah," I said. "I think I'm going to like it here. Did Jordan tell you he got a job?"

"Oh, yes, at the UPS Store, right? He'll be fine. He'll like that. He's good with people."

"Yeah," I said. I wondered what I was going to do. I thought about the different restaurants in town, and also my old music teacher and the music store he owned.

"What are your plans?" Stan asked as if he read my mind.

"I usually... I sometimes play my violin for tips in restaurants," I said. "Or wait tables."

"Oh, you play the violin?" he asked. "Jordan didn't mention that. You'll have to play in church! We love for our musically gifted brethren to grace us with their talents."

"Oh, yeah, sure," I said. "How did Jordan find your church?" It was something I'd wondered about for a while. Stan's church, located in a strip mall, had once been a barbershop, which they had gutted and fitted out like a hotel meeting room. Blue industrial carpet, beige paint, a few pictures of Jesus on the walls, and a makeshift pulpit. Folding chairs. What it lacked in amenities it made up for in sincerity. Stan—Pastor Stan the people called him—served coffee and homemade cookies after services and held Bible study at home. To keep the church going, they held fundraisers, car washes, and sold self-published books on the Internet. Apparently, they got a deal on the rent from the strip mall.

"Well," Stan said, "I have a prison ministry and see men from the penitentiary who are in rehab. Often, I minister to their needs as they transition from prison to civilian life."

"I see," I said, watching Jordan out of the corner of my eye.

"You know, Jordan told me about the accident that led to his imprisonment," he said. "I understand you left shortly afterward." His eyes seemed intense and penetrating. I had no idea what story he'd heard.

"I went to Hazelden for rehab," I told him.

"Yes, he mentioned that. I wonder if you'd like to get together sometime and talk about the difference between moving on and running away?" He looked concerned, with just the right note of pastoral caring.

"Yeah, maybe," I said, thinking that he was someone I didn't want to alienate if he was helping Jordan.

"You just let me know. Maybe we can slow down that rolling stone, huh?"

I smiled. "Maybe."

Jordan came up behind me. "Isn't he great?" he gushed, looking at Stan. "Stan has been my rock, Coop. He helped me to see that we could get out from under the sin we've been living in and find our way to good things. I promised him I'd be faithful, and he promised he'd guide me once I got out. He helped me find this place."

"I like to have my parishioners close by," said Stan. "It helps me keep an eye on my little flock." He had a wide white smile and uncomplicated brown eyes. I thought he probably cared about Jordan, and that was good enough for me.

"I am so grateful to have this second chance," said Jordan sincerely, and I put my hand on his arm to give it a squeeze.

He smiled at me then, the same smile he used to give me when we were kids and found three dollars in change under the couch cushions to buy candy.

"I'm going to make lemonade," I said, retreating to the kitchen. I wanted something to do. I was cutting lemons when the phone rang. "Hello?" I answered.

"Yay! You're in, aren't you?" *My sister, Julie.*

"Jules, how's it going?"

"Better now that my brother's got a place to live in town." She paused. "Have you got any idea what you're going to do?"

"You mean like a job?" I asked. The noise from the living room was filtering in and I found it hard to hear her.

"Yeah," she said. "Dad hoped you'd work at the firm, I guess, if music didn't work out."

"I'm no accountant," I told her. "I couldn't be any more useless at anything than that. I thought I'd go see the manager at Mama Lina's. I've waited tables and I've played for tips in a lot of Italian places."

"You're going to play for tips? You got into Juilliard, Cooper, surely that must mean…"

"I'll go back to school as soon as I can, Jules, I've thought about it. But it takes time and cash I don't have yet. In order to do anything with music I need a graduate degree."

"Maybe you can teach violin," she suggested.

"Maybe," I said, but privately I didn't think anyone in this small town would let me near their kids.

"You'll look into it?"

"Yes, of course I will." I scooped powdered sugar into a pitcher of water and added lemon juice and zest. "I'd planned to all along."

"Okay." She sighed. "I love you."

"Love you too."

"Cooper?" she asked quietly.

"Yes?"

"I didn't do wrong, giving Jordie your number, did I?" She hesitated. "That was okay, right?"

I leaned my head against the wall, which felt cool and soothing against what was becoming a monster headache. "Sure, Jules, I needed to make this right. I'm glad you gave him my number." How many lies would I have to tell, I wondered, before I believed them myself?

* * *

The doorbell rang and as soon as I brought the pizza boxes in and paid, everyone fell on the food. Stan cleared his throat and said a nice long prayer, during which I thought I saw Jordan pinching off bits of his toppings and eating them. I smiled. Some things never changed. After I got my pizza, I poured everyone lemonade. We all sat around, eating and talking quietly together.

At the end of the evening, Jordie and I said good-bye to his friends. He closed the door behind Stan, who was the last to leave.

"Hey," he said shyly.

"Hey." I smiled. Crap, I was tired. I started to pick up paper plates, napkins, cups, and trash from the living room floor. Jordan leaned against the wall, watching me.

"This is weird, huh?"

"Yeah, a little. But it's just us, Jordie, like always." I tossed some things into the tiny plastic trash bin under the sink. "We'll need a bigger trash bin for the kitchen, I think."

"Have you ever lived in a place like this?" he asked.

"No," I answered truthfully. "I've pretty much lived on the streets for the last three years."

"Oh, *Coop.*" Jordan sat down on the couch.

I went to sit next to him. "I mostly roamed around, you know? I'd find places to play for tips, then go to cheap motels when I had enough cash. Otherwise, I slept in parks and camped on the beach. The last month or so I've been staying in a room above a bar."

"A bar?" he asked. "Wasn't that hard? All that booze?"

"No."

"I can't imagine."

"Anyway, they let me stay there in a studio apartment, and I helped in the kitchen and played for people during peak times in the restaurant. It was a good place." I felt myself falling into the memories a little. Into the warmth that even now I felt when I thought of St. Nacho's.

"I see," he said. "Did you live with your guy then?"

"No," I said. "It was a studio; I lived alone."

"So this is your first time living with someone?"

"Yes," I answered. "Since I lived at home."

He put his head on the back of the couch and chuckled. "I promise I won't welcome you the way I got 'welcomed' in prison."

"Jordie," I breathed. It was as if I could *feel* my heart breaking.

"No, it's nothing." He shook his head. "Nothing I didn't already do, right?"

"Jordan, I—"

"Really," he interrupted, shaking his head. "It's all in the past, Cooper. You want the first shower?"

"No," I said. "You go on."

He hesitated. "I hope you won't think… I want to ask you for a favor. I'm not used to being alone at night. I wondered if you'd come and sleep… I mean, just sleep, okay? In the bedroom with me."

"Jordie," I said, not knowing what the hell to do.

"I won't be, like, you know… I won't expect anything. I just want to be close. You know, a warm body. I wake up scared a lot."

"Oh." I thought about it. "Okay, I guess."

Jordan's face was transformed by a bright smile. "Thanks, Cooper. I love you. You know that, right?"

"Yeah," I said. He held his fist out for me and I punched it. "I know. I'm here for you, okay?"

"Yes." He got up to take his shower. "I know, Coop."

I got up, moved my four boxes to the bedroom, and hung up my clothes with his. I worried then that we'd be living together in every way that counts as soon as he could find a way to rationalize it and convince me. I knew that I was basically weak and more than a little lonely.

Jordie was my best friend; he'd been my lover from the first second I'd realized I was gay. My lover, my best friend, and my "partner in crime." I'd have been less than honest if I said we'd been exclusive. We'd roamed the streets of tiny River Falls at the top of the food chain, taking whomever and whatever we'd wanted. Our partnership had been so solid that when I'd left for Juilliard I knew Jordie would always be there for me, whenever I needed him. I left and never looked back. I hadn't known that someday I would want something different.

I didn't expect to see Shawn again. A guy like Shawn could move on, and Jordie offered warmth and security and the press of human flesh. I knew it wouldn't take me too much time succumb to him, because I'd learned long since to take what comfort life offered and live with it.

I wondered at the time, though, what Jordan had learned.

Chapter Eleven

The small city of River Falls, Wisconsin, where I grew up had grown considerably since my childhood. Once a tiny town that boasted a state normal school for teachers, it was now a bedroom community of St. Paul, a short drive across the border from neighboring Minnesota.

It still had only two stoplights, one at the beginning of Main Street, and the other, predictably, at the end. While it now had more suburban tract houses, and a number of chain fast-food restaurants, Mama Lina's Ristorante Italiano, unchanged since my grandparents' courting days, still occupied its cavernous place on Main Street between the movie theater and what was once the Sears Catalog store.

I entered the front door during the lull between lunch and dinner and was told to wait until Jefferson, the grandson of the original Mama Lina, was ready to speak with me.

I remembered Jefferson from high school, primarily because Julie once had a crush on him. He hadn't been interested though, and had taken some other girl out for most of his days as an RFHS Wildcat. I hadn't heard anything about him since. Julie had moved on to college and older boys who liked her just fine.

"Cooper Wyatt," said a voice from the hallway behind the bar. "Come back here, if you don't mind, to my office." Jefferson had changed little, his boyish face passive as he ushered me into a small room with a desk. Framed photos of notables dining in Mama Lina's red vinyl booths, including Minnesota's famous governor, Jesse Ventura, hung on the walls. "I hadn't heard you were back in town."

I didn't know what to say to that. I didn't suppose anyone cared whether I was back in town enough to actually talk about it. "I haven't been back long."

"I see," he said. "I see Julie around every now and then," he added, and I wondered if he regretted blowing off my sister's crush. More than one man in this town had eyes for my beautiful, and now very successful, sister.

I genuinely smiled when I thought of Jules. "It's been good to be with her." She'd sent someone to Mama Lina's the day before to get me an application to fill out.

"I think her coffeehouse is just about the hippest place to be in River Falls," he said. "You can't get near it on a Friday night. Folks come from a ways away. Are you working there?"

"Uh, no. That's what I wanted to talk to you about, actually," I said. I refused point blank to work for my sister. If my past in this town was going to embarrass my family, the least I could do was not take it to their doorstep. "I wondered, since I have culinary arts training, if you might have a place for me here?"

"Oh. Here?" he asked. I could see his brows come together in the middle. "Well."

"The last job I had, at Nacho's Bar in California, I did food prep in the kitchen until the peak hours, and then played the violin from table to table for tips. People seemed to think…" I pushed the application, which I'd painstakingly filled out, toward him. "It's all there, restaurants I've worked in, places I've played."

He did a double take when he saw my cramped writing. "Wow, you've moved around a lot. What kind of music did you play?" He seemed at least a little interested.

"I played customer requests. Love songs, "Happy Birthday," mariachi music, Irish folk songs. Whatever. You know, I was there to amuse the crowd. They liked me."

"I see." He steepled his fingers. "You know lots of songs, I presume?"

"Yes," I said. "And a lot of classical music."

"It's going to be hard. People have long memories."

"I know."

"It might not be the best thing that you returned, you know? Jordan Jensen is back as well."

"I know." I held my breath.

"Is that why you're here?" he asked. "Because Jordan got out?"

I hesitated. It wouldn't do to prevaricate about something that would so quickly become small-town gossip. "Yes, he and I are staying together."

Jefferson shook his head. "People hate him for what he did. You would be wise to distance yourself."

"I was there, Jefferson," I said. "I can't."

"It's not the same. No one thinks it's the same."

I remained silent. Jefferson drummed his fingers on the table and for some absurd reason it reminded me of the first *Godfather* movie. I waited for him to tell me I owed him a favor in the future.

"If you want, you can start in the kitchen tomorrow, the four until closing shift." He shuffled some papers on his desk. "It's up to you whether you want to try to play the violin for tips, but the people of this town haven't forgotten or forgiven Jordan, and as soon as they're aware of your current association you will be held similarly in contempt."

I sighed. "I understand."

"I like your family, Cooper. I don't want to see you hurt."

"It's all right. Maybe it would be best if I stayed in the kitchen, but frankly, I get good tips when I play the violin, and I could use the cash."

"That's fine. However, if there's trouble, I'll ask you to leave."

"Certainly." I stood and shook hands with Jefferson. "Thank you."

"Thank *you*. I can always use good kitchen help. I'll see you tomorrow." He saw me to the door of his office, and I left feeling better than I had since I'd gotten to River Falls. And worse. I was running out of money, and the prospect of a job buoyed my sagging spirits. But if my association with Jordan was a problem, I wasn't likely to solve it by walking down Main Street playing my violin.

I got home to the apartment and tossed my keys on the kitchen counter next to the tiny, old microwave Julie had found for us when we moved in. I heated water to make tea, and when I had it made took it to the balcony where I could smoke.

The sun was beginning to slip over the building and by dinner it would beat down fully on the small plastic table and chairs Jordan and I had purchased. Already the heat and humidity wilted me, and at dusk the mosquitoes would eat me alive. Morning was the best time of the day, and Jordan enjoyed it most when I cooked breakfast and set it out on the wobbly little picnic table.

I discovered that prison had done nothing for Jordan's cooking skills, so I did most of that. I liked it. I'd never had that before, the homely duty of seeing meals on the table for myself and someone else. Often friends from church would drop by and bring casseroles or a salad and bread, and we'd share. I thought I would have liked it, but for the fact that I missed Shawn and my friends in California.

Jordan slept fitfully when he slept at all. He had the capacity to stay up rather late, fueled by a large intake of coffee, which often left him watching television or chatting with friends after I went to sleep. I was thinking I ought to let him have me if it would help him sleep.

No, *that wasn't all I was thinking*. I was thinking that I was here, and I was trying to live with the man, and I needed it as much as he did. After everything I'd had with Shawn. How sick was that?

The doorbell rang. I got up and opened the door to find Stan waiting patiently.

"Hello," I said, moving back to let him in.

"Hello, Cooper," he said. "I hoped I'd find you at home."

I smiled. "Jordan's out," I said. "He's still at work."

"It was you I wanted to see," said Stan, staring. It felt uncomfortable having him here when Jordan was away, but I couldn't quite put my finger on why. He stood on the threshold, his youngish face placid. He was wearing a blue golf shirt and the kind of jeans I associate with older men who aren't comfortable in denim. They were creased. I invited him to have a seat on the couch.

"Can I get you something to drink?" I asked. "I'm having tea."

"That would be nice, thank you."

I set the water to boil and went to get my own off the patio.

"I wanted to talk to you about your plans here in River Falls," he began when I returned. Once again I regretted not having a chair. I sat down on the couch next to him.

"Have you given any thought to what you're going to do?"

"I got a job at Mama Lina's, in the kitchen," I said. "I plan on going to UWRF, when I can get in, for music in order to finish my degree."

"I understand you used to play in the St. Croix River Valley Orchestra?"

"Where'd you hear that?" I asked, surprised. "Yes. I did." I swallowed hard. I had been their youngest member and concertmaster.

"I found it in the newspapers," he said. I flushed. He must have seen everything. "You were quite a prodigy," he remarked.

"I don't know," I said.

"No need to be modest," he said, conspiratorially slipping closer on the couch. He slid an arm behind my shoulders, experimentally, I thought. I frowned, and he pulled back a little. "Juilliard," he said. "That was something."

"Well, I failed at that, didn't I?"

"What happened?" he asked.

"Partied a little too much," I said. "I got bad grades, missed a couple of important events." *Like recitals*, I thought, *like the whole second semester of my freshman year.* I wished he'd never brought it up. The chime from the microwave sounded and I got up to make him tea. "Tension Tamer or Sleepytime?" I asked him.

He chuckled as though I'd said something funny. "I think Tension Tamer."

"Do you like it sweetened?"

"No, thank you." I put the tea in front of him, but he didn't touch it. "I'll come right to the point then," he said, leaning in again. "I like you, Cooper, and I want to see to it that you get off to a healthy start here in town."

"Thank you."

"And as you know, I have a number of people in my flock who have made some poor choices. The Lord doesn't hold us accountable once we repent. You know that, don't you?" he asked, his eyes boring into mine.

"I guess."

"Then you know that if you're willing to make a true and proper repentance, not only will the Lord forgive you, but he'll remember your sin no more." He slid his arm back around my shoulders again, and I couldn't think clearly, I was so focused on that.

"Yes."

"The Lord knows your heart, son," he said, and I thought at the time, he wasn't that much older than me. "He knows you didn't mean to be the instrument of that child's death."

"I—"

"He knows you couldn't help yourself, that drink was strong upon you and you forfeited your agency to—"

"Wait," I said, getting up off the couch so fast my head felt a little light. "I don't know what you think happened, but—"

"I only know what Jordan told me. That you were too drunk to drive and Jordan took your keys away and took the wheel to stop you from driving drunk."

"He what?" I asked. That wasn't exactly how I remembered it.

"I'm sure Jordan isn't sorry for taking responsibility like that. It's cost him a lot, and he's not done paying yet, but I'm certain he feels it was worth it. Privately, he's told me that he felt good to be able to save you from suffering that."

I blinked. I'm sure I couldn't have spoken if I'd wanted to.

"Jordan is a very special man, Cooper. He's become extremely important to me, to my ministry." He took a tentative sip of his tea. "Men like Jordan need guidance, discipline. They need structure."

"I see," I said.

"He comes to me for that," said Stan. "I find I rather feel that you might need guidance and counseling as well."

"I don't," I said. I leaned against the wall opposite him.

"We'll see," said Stan, continuing to drink his tea as if he had all the time in the world.

"I don't," I repeated. He shrugged.

"Nevertheless," he said. "The Lord has punished you and will continue to punish you until you take responsibility for your actions and come to Him in repentance."

I swallowed hard. I didn't know what to say, but I heard the key in the door signaling Jordan's arrival, and I turned to greet him.

"Hey," I said. He stood for a minute in the polo shirt with the UPS Store logo on it. He had little pieces of packing peanuts in his hair and they clung to him, presumably because of static electricity. They looked like enormous dandruff.

"Hey." He tossed his keys down next to mine. "What's up?"

"I was just talking to Cooper about coming to the Lord with his burdens," Stan said, still sipping his tea. "Like you have."

Jordan looked at me, I thought, in a considering way. "Maybe you should, Coop," he said. "Maybe you need to bring it to the Savior. It might help with the car thing."

"What car thing?" asked Stan.

"It's nothing," I said, quickly. I glared at Jordie, telling him with my eyes that he was an asshole to bring that up as I brushed the Styrofoam pellets off his hair.

"Cooper is afraid to get into a car anymore."

"Is this true?" asked Stan, all solicitous concern.

I kept my eyes on Jordan, and he glared back at me. "Yes," I said.

"It's going to become a problem you can't ignore when it starts snowing, Cooper," Jordan warned.

"He's right," said Stan. "What happens when you get in a car?"

"It's just a phobia," I said. "I'll handle it. Anyway, Mama Lina's is within walking distance."

"In the winter you'd better plan on cross-country skiing," Jordan said.

"I can ski." I sounded petulant.

"Your instrument is going to love the drastic temperature change." He got a Pepsi out of the fridge and twisted off the cap. It foamed over and he cursed, jumping and holding it away from his body. "Shit."

"Here, babe," I said, getting a towel. I helped him wipe up the spill. He kissed me in front of Stan. I was surprised and did the eye-roll thing. He shrugged.

"Stan knows we're a couple," said Jordan, and Stan nodded. *I didn't know we were a couple.*

"That's why I'm taking a particular interest in you, Cooper," he said in a silky voice that grated on my nerves. "We must do everything we can, mustn't we, Jordan, to see that Cooper here feels the love of the Lord."

"Yes, sir," said Jordan. His eyes shone at Stan's words.

"Starting with this car business. I'm going to read up about phobias and do some serious praying, Cooper, and I'll be in touch." He gave me my mug back, and then hugged Jordan to him tightly. "Jordan, I'll see you tonight, all right?"

"All right," Jordan agreed. Stan left.

"Is there Bible study tonight?" I asked. I was starting to get things out of the fridge for dinner. I'd dropped by the food mart and picked up some fresh vegetables and chicken for a quick stir-fry. I had brown rice from the night before all ready to go. "I can have dinner on in twenty, if you want to grab a quick shower."

"It's not Bible study," said Jordan as he left for the bedroom. "It's pastoral counseling. I sometimes need to talk to Stan about things." He hovered in the doorway. I put down the chef's knife, my one splurge since arriving in River Falls.

"What kind of things?" I had to admit I didn't care to be the subject of their conversations.

Jordan looked down. "He says it's the stages of grief. He says what I'm feeling, guilt, anger, and depression, are normal things. That I just have to deal with my feelings in a healthy way and work through them."

"I guess that's right," I said. "That sounds pretty smart."

He beamed at me. "Stan's really a great guy. He understands."

I smiled. "I'm glad."

"You want to join me?" he asked, kind of grinning, nodding toward the shower.

I froze. "I can't, babe," I said. "Sorry. I have to see that you get a good meal before you go, don't I?" I smiled at him.

"Yeah." He didn't smile back. "Thanks." He turned and went into the bathroom and I heard the water turn on. I let out the breath I'd been holding since I'd opened the door to Stan.

Chapter Twelve

The first opportunity I had to play violin for the patrons of Mama Lina's was two Sundays after I started working there. I went, at Jefferson's invitation, to play on my day off. I swallowed my nerves in his little office, along with several aspirin and an expensive blue bottle of water that he graciously gave me. Then I took my instrument to play for his guests, many of whom I'd grown up with, and many of whom reviled me as a sexual deviant and killer of children. I started at a table in the corner, alerted by a waitress named Beth that the customer was having a birthday. I played "Happy Birthday," and because they didn't stone me, I played the "Tarantella" as well.

By noon, I had relaxed enough to enjoy what was left of the morning, despite my headache. I was recognized, but no one seemed to have any feelings about me other than to wonder what I'd been doing. It seemed the memory of my playing remained, especially for those who had been in school with me. I had been an insufferable show-off, I knew, but no one held it against me. I went from table to table taking requests, playing love songs, folk songs, and the occasional outrageous request, like "Kashmir" by Led Zeppelin. I delivered, even on the absurd. Several people threatened to tell my old music instructor, Mr. Larsen, that I was back in town and playing at Mama's, and I shuddered with apprehension. I originally thought I'd see if I could work in his music store, but then, realizing what a huge disappointment I must have been, I couldn't find the courage.

Sooner or later he was going to walk into the restaurant, though, because everyone over thirty did, and sooner or later, I'd be chopping his vegetables as well. I would have to swallow my pride and accept his disillusionment as well as my own. I did rather good trade, though, and made enough in tips to pay for food for Jordan and me for the whole week. Added to the pasta dishes and salads Jefferson let me take home on the days that I worked, I was going to be able to treat Jordie to a movie or maybe even a ball game in the cities.

I left Mama's in a fairly good mood. When I got back to the apartment, the church contingent was there.

"We missed you at services today," said Stan.

"I'm sorry, I was working." I put my violin in the coat closet. For some reason I didn't want to go too deeply into what I was doing. Stan followed me into the kitchen where I washed my hands and started to make a salad.

"Have you thought anymore about what we talked about the other day?" he asked me. "About joining the church formally and coming to me for counseling?"

I *had* thought about whether to join in and be part of Stan's flock. It would require finding sincerity on my part and full-immersion baptism, two things I didn't think I could do. On the one hand, he was there for Jordan, someone for Jordan to cling to when he felt overwhelmed by the newness of living back among the good people of River Falls. He seemed to be a good man. On the other, I found myself feeling short of breath whenever he was around. Like something was surrounding me, trying to smother me.

"I don't think I have any kind of religious calling," I said.

He watched me closely, waiting for me to continue. When I didn't, I think he felt he had to change tactics. "What are you going to do, though? What's going to happen when you're tempted by drugs or alcohol, or you have a crisis and you need to deal with it sober?"

I shook my head. "I've been sober for over three years. I won't be relapsing." I knew that, at least.

"People say that, but they can never run far enough or fast enough that it doesn't catch up. You have to have a plan in place. A strategy. You can't do it alone."

"What you say is true, but—"

"I can see you're not ready to hear what I have to say right now, Cooper. I'm sorry, but I'm going to keep saying it." He put a firm hand on my shoulder and squeezed it. He had warm eyes and a nice smile with big teeth that I suspected were capped. But when he talked to me I just felt dragged into something that I genuinely wanted to avoid. Sooner or later, I'd have to make a choice.

I felt tired and excused myself for a while. I showered, realizing that what I wanted most of all was to get away, to take a long walk, maybe to my sister's coffeehouse. She was likely to be there right in the thick of things, and I found I missed her. I dressed and when I returned to the living room, I had to wait a minute for Stan to finish an earnest prayer.

"...Blessings on this home that both men who live here might find the forgiveness they need, in their own hearts and in the hearts of those they wronged. Amen."

My face burned. "I'm going to go see Julie."

"I thought you were going to eat with us." Jordan got to his feet. Several pairs of eyes stared at me.

"I guess I'm just restless after my big debut at Mama Lina's." I made it a joke. "I want to see my sister. I know she'll be holding court at Grounds." I kissed Jordan's cheek, and then wondered if it was overkill.

He smiled. "See you later then, yeah?"

"Yeah," I said, getting my keys and heading out the door.

"We'll talk soon," said Stan, and I nodded.

* * *

At one time, I imagined, I had every crack in every formed concrete block of the downtown sidewalk of River Falls memorized—enough to walk it blindfolded, even now. Newer cars were parked in the diagonal parking designations. Nicer cars, I noted, pricier than the salt-pitted American models that had dotted the street when I was very young. Hallowed Grounds was on the corner of Main Street and Bear Lake Lane, just a ten-minute walk from my apartment. I was coming at it from the east and had to pass the Ben Franklin and the public library to get to it. I continued at the desultory pace I realized I'd started using since I got back home. Time slowed in River Falls too, although not like it did in Santo Ignacio with its kind of magical healing quality. It faltered, like aging, like sore joints, muscle weakness, and loss of bone density. I felt shrunken in River Falls, where in Santo Ignacio I'd had the feeling of getting larger.

I took a look in the window of the public library and noticed it was open on Sundays now. I stopped to watch as a group of children sat in a semicircle on an alphabet rug waiting for the librarian to tell a story, their mothers sitting in chairs behind them. The librarian held up the book and introduced it, I thought, handing it off to a helper, who showed the pictures. When she began to tell the story, she both spoke and signed it, like Shawn, enthusiastically using her whole body. I followed my feet into the children's area of the library before my brain even engaged and sat to watch her. There was something so sweetly familiar about her fluttering hands. To find a part of the life I'd left behind in St. Nacho's here in River Falls, where I felt like an exile, washed over me like warm light. I was every bit as enraptured as the children were.

"I couldn't help but notice you don't have children with you," the librarian remarked after the kids ran off with their parents to find books. "A big story hour fan, are you?"

"No." I'm sure I blushed. "No."

"Come off it, Cooper. Don't say you don't recognize me. I'll be devastated."

I stared at her, appalled. I didn't recognize her. Shit. *Shit.*

Her silvery laugh was not quiet enough to go unnoticed in the library, and people looked over at us.

She shook her head. "Dang, I tried everything to get your attention when I was a kid at RFHS. I played the viola?"

I shook my head.

"When you were a senior and I was a junior? Mary Lynn Anders, now Johnson." She stuck her hand out and I shook it.

"Girls…weren't my thing," I said. "I'm afraid."

"I get that—now. I'm glad to see you anyway," she said. "So I take it that it isn't regret for failing to notice my otherworldly beauty that draws you here?"

I laughed. I wish I had noticed her. She seemed nice. "Sorry," I said. "I saw you signing. I have a friend… I was trying to learn sign language before I came back to River Falls."

"I see," she said.

"Anyway, I like watching it. I mean, when people talk with their hands. I find it…attractive. That sounds stupid."

"No, I do too. It's one of the reasons I learned. That and my first nephew was born deaf. He likes a good story too." She smiled.

"My friend wasn't born deaf, so he speaks. I just…sometimes I think I'd like to talk to him like that, instead of me texting and him answering with his voice or me writing and him reading. It's exciting when people talk with their hands."

"I know. It's so graceful and way more immediate."

"I was wondering… Maybe I could volunteer or something. Clean? Wash your car? Maybe you could teach me." *How stupid is that? Am I still holding out hope I'll see Shawn again?*

"Oh, sure, I could teach you some. You don't have to clean or anything, but frankly, I could use some help with my laundry." I'm sure she saw something flicker in my eyes because she laughed hard. "Kidding. Just kidding. Were you always this awkward?"

"Yes," I said. I resolved that I liked her and wanted to tell her only the truth. "I was, but I hid it behind a shitload of partying."

Her face suddenly sobered, and I felt like all the air was sucked out of the room. "I remember."

"I'm done with all that."

"I'm glad." She smiled again. "Stop by the library in the morning tomorrow. I'll bring you some books." She began to walk toward the circulation desk, where a bunch of impatient preschoolers waited for her. "Right now I have more important customers."

"Tomorrow morning." I grinned at her and left the building. Mary Lynn, viola. Still wasn't ringing any bells. Shit. *How many nice people had I just completely ignored?* I was still frowning in thought when I got to Hallowed Grounds.

I saw my sister right away, schmoozing the caffeinated faithful at the register. She immediately stopped what she was doing when she saw me and came around the counter for a hug. She ordered us both something in white ceramic cups as large as a soccer balls and sat down with me at a tiny bistro table. One of her minions brought peanut butter brownies.

"It is *good* to be you," I said, looking around at her store. Everywhere I looked an eclectic mix of modern, gothic, and

Victorian furnishings cluttered the small space, spilling out right onto the sidewalk, where the doors opened and she had set out tables. She had wall racks full of trinkets for sale, as well as art by local artists, jewelry, books, and greeting cards. The food looked fabulous. She had a long white marble counter, copper cappuccino machines, and overstuffed divans and club chairs with tiny marble tables that made it look like a picture of a Parisian cafe in the 1930s.

Julie was a hell of an entrepreneur, but the most surprising thing was that it went over as well as it did in stodgy River Falls, where a John Deere baseball cap got you into the finest places, the men were men, and guys like me left home early and often.

"I'll tell you a secret. I'm already playing a complicated game of Go with the appliance place next door. They don't know it yet, but I've surrounded them and choked off any chance for retreat. Well, that and the owners are old and looking to buy a casita in Arizona. By next fall at the latest, Hallowed Grounds will be four times the size it is now." She read my surprise. "It's changing here. More people have come from the cities. Kids from the high school love this place. I like having a place they can come for an alternative to drinking beer in the school parking lot."

I burned with shame.

"Oh, baby... I didn't mean... Well, yes, I did, I guess." She stuck up her chin. "I'd rather they get high on caffeine here and read bad poetry than get into the kind of trouble you did."

Well, it might not have worked on Jordie and me, but I had to give her credit. "I love you," I said. "In case I haven't told you lately." *Where had that come from?*

She smiled. "Me too."

"So," I said. "I played at Mama Lina's this morning."

"I've already overheard people talking about you. You've made quite an impression."

"Yeah?" I asked. "Good or bad?"

"All good. The general consensus is that you have come back, at last, with a renewed determination to become what you should have been all along."

"I see," I said.

She caught my hand in hers and gave it a brief squeeze. "I always saw you on a detour, Cooper, not on a road of no return."

I sighed. "I don't know what it was."

"Look," she said, gripping her cup and taking a sip. I didn't tell her there was a blob of foam on her nose. *Some things never change.* "There was a time when I didn't feel I could be straight with you, but now I'm wondering if that was just as bad as being honest and alienating you completely."

"I find people who were 'straight' with me didn't make much of a dent back in the day."

"You weren't going to tell me I had foam on my nose, were you?" She grinned.

"What, is that some kind of a test?"

"No, there's a mirror behind you and I just noticed."

"Oh."

She sighed. "How's it going, Cooper?" she asked. "Really."

"I miss California sometimes," I said carefully. "I liked Santo Ignacio. Something about me changed there."

"What do you mean?"

"I don't know. Like something softening me up and warming me, from the inside out." *Could I ever find the words for that?* "It was a healing place."

She was silent for a while. "Was it pretty there?"

"Yeah, a lot like the Oregon coast. Unspoiled."

"Must have been nice."

"It was." I pulled off a corner of my brownie and ate it. It was so good I couldn't think of anything else for a minute. "I was sorry to leave it."

"Why did you?" she asked suddenly, leaning forward.

"What?"

"I didn't give Jordan your number so you would come back here and take up where you left off with him."

"It's hardly like we're where we left off, though, is it?"

"Of course not, how could it be?" she asked. "But what I didn't expect is you moving back to town and taking up with him again."

"He needs me," I said. "It wasn't easy for him to come back, to face the people here alone."

She was silent for a long time. "I wouldn't be honest if I didn't tell you I want you to put your past behind you once and for all."

"People can't just put their pasts behind them, Jules. I've spent almost four years on the road, running, and it still caught up with me."

"I think…" she said, toying with my brownie. "I think, if you ever figure out what is *your* past and what isn't, and stop getting it all mixed up with Jordan's, you'll be free of it."

"I'll never be free of it, Julie. And anyway, I can't do that. My past is mixed with Jordan's, whether I want it to be or not. He paid the price for something we both did."

Her hand came down on the table with a bang that caused our coffee cups to jump and people all around to startle. "Actions count," she said. "What you *did* counts, and what you *didn't do* counts. And nothing Jordan said then or now can change that if you don't let it. You can't go on feeling responsible for something you didn't do, Coop."

"But I am responsible. I did nothing to stop him. Sure, I knew I couldn't drive, but I didn't do anything to stop him from driving! It isn't that simple. I gave up responsibility to him not because I was a good person or because I knew better than to drive drunk. I did it because I wanted to…be a passenger. Let somebody else think for me. I picked the wrong person. I know now that was as bad as if I'd driven myself. I don't even want to think about this anymore."

"I *want* you to think about it, Coop. I want you to think and think and *think* about it, because I believe you'll realize that we can only be responsible for what we do, all by ourselves. That seems like it's enough responsibility for anyone."

"And what if we were all to abdicate our responsibility? Excuse ourselves from the process and just let others take the fall?"

She put her hand on mine and squeezed, and I could see the caring and the anxiety in her eyes. I wondered if I'd ever see her look at me without that pain again.

I ended up leaving after we finished our coffee in a strained silence and walked back to the apartment deep in thought. I looked in the library window and saw Mary Lynn packing up puzzles and games, and I wondered again if the real world might just be somewhere between the uncomplicated one my sister described and the indecipherable and frightening place I had always believed it to be.

Chapter Thirteen

When I got home the only people left in the apartment were Stan and Jordan. I said a polite hello, but they seemed to be in deep conversation, so I went onto the balcony to smoke. Jordan seemed agitated, and Stan was using that supercilious, smooth voice of his to calm him. It wasn't long before Jordan came to the slider and opened it.

"I'm going to go with Stan for a while. He thinks I need a meeting."

"Are you okay?" I asked. I knew Jordan attended regular AA meetings. He was years past his "thirty meetings in thirty days," but often went every day anyway.

"Yeah." He sighed, raking his hand through his hair. "I don't know. I'm...I'm just going, okay?"

"Okay." I watched him walk across the living room with Stan and out the front door. Stan turned to me and gave me a look that was hard to decipher. I wondered if he thought maybe I was bad for Jordan. It wouldn't have surprised me, given what he'd said about the accident. It didn't matter. I finished my cigarette and went back inside, where I found the kitchen full of the effects of that afternoon's meal, and I took the time to clean it up.

* * *

All in all, I liked the quiet of our apartment, yet I knew that Jordan was unhappy that we didn't have a television. I liked to take walks, and he liked to stay indoors. I think my practicing got on his nerves. I tolerated the church group, went to AA meetings, and attended Bible study. I knew he was aware that I didn't have any kind of personal spiritual calling, but I didn't see it as "going through the motions" the way he thought I did. I tried to give him space and stability. He routinely found reasons to call Stan for counseling and searched for meetings to attend. He always needed more.

At some point, I began to go to the library often to help out with cleaning or whatever Mary Lynn might need. She taught me some basic sign language, enough so that I could carry on a greeting and a small discussion of the weather. She gave me books, and I practiced with a couple of DVDs when I could watch them on the library players. I memorized signed words, but was unable yet to place them into coherent sentences.

Jordan tolerated my interest, saying that it would be good to have someone who could sign for Stan later if the church attracted any deaf parishioners. I walked past the banks of computers in the library every day, avoiding the temptation to use them to reconnect with Santo Ignacio. But my fingers itched to reach out for something, *anything* that would bring Shawn's face more clearly to my mind.

Summer hung thick and heavy on us; the humidity and mosquitoes were taking their toll. I was sitting in the church with the usual group, listening to Stan talk on and on about sin and redemption, a message I'd heard him give a number of times before. I looked at Jordan. He watched Stan so earnestly. I remembered the many times when we were kids when Jordie had had that same enraptured look on his face. I still found it as endearing as I found it heartbreaking.

I knew then that I had been wading through the humid days marking time. Jordie had a new drug of choice in the person of Pastor Stan, and I wasn't going to be able, this time, to share it with him.

I wondered what Shawn was doing all the time now. Was he working full-time during the summer or did he have classes? Would he be sunning himself on the beach with his friends? Would he be picnicking in the evenings with Kevin by the light of his little battery-powered camping lantern? I could see him in my mind with his gray rubber tub of dishes, wiping off tables and throwing that smile—that impossibly bright, beautiful smile—around Nacho's bar. I knew so little about him and I'd told him less about me, yet I think he understood me better than most everyone here who'd known me all my life.

* * *

I ambled down Main Street toward the library and Mary Lynn. More and more, I took refuge in the silence there. It might have been the only place in River Falls where I didn't feel I owed anyone an explanation. I bought a coffee to go for myself and one for Mary Lynn, and crossed Veterans Park. The fountain burbled busily and there were birds scattered around, eating birdseed that I suspected Yarnista owner and avid needlewoman, Sally Lindstrom, put out in the morning before anyone else was up. I'd never caught her at it. I suspected her because she always watched the birds from the front window of her shop when she was bored.

I passed the memorial and was walking by the benches, and there was Shawn. Sitting. On a bench. *In my hometown.* With his eyes closed, allowing the sun to warm his amazing upturned face.

Well, *damn.* Everything can change in an instant. I'd always believed it to be one of the great truths. But now, for the second time in my life, it had happened to *me.*

I sat down next to Shawn and he opened his eyes. The moment he saw me, they lit with a mixture of emotions it would take even the experts at Yarnista a lifetime to untangle. I saw surprise and more than a little annoyance as he slapped his spare phone into my hands.

"You didn't *even* tell me where you were going," he said. "I discovered that I resent that. A lot."

"I thought," I began to say, confused, and then realized I had to type it. I texted, *I thought you understood. I had to come back for someone else. I know I told you that Jordan needed me. That I couldn't still be with you and come back and be here for him.*

He grinned at me, and I wanted to put my hands on his face. His touch would be warmth and color and vibrant life in a place where I'd been feeling all that choked out of me. I swallowed hard. Those amber eyes sparkled for me. He reached out, I thought, to brush my hair back. Instead he thumbed the barbell piercing on my eyebrow.

"I never heard you say a word about any of that."

What could I say? He had me there.

Shawn put his hands behind his head and leaned back, once again with his eyes closed, absorbing the summer morning. I nudged him with my shoulder and gave him Mary Lynn's coffee. It wasn't strange at all, sipping our coffee in mutual silence. It was the strongest feeling that I've ever had: that *rightness* that we shared in mutual silence. We stayed like that for a long time until a shadow fell over our faces.

"Hello, Cooper," said Pastor Stan. I looked up and had to put my hand to my eyes because he was backlit by the sun.

"Hi, Stan," I said, standing up. Shawn stood with me, and I could feel his hand at the small of my back. Stan was looking at Shawn and me expectantly.

"Stan, this is Shawn, a friend of mine from California." To Shawn I said, "This is Stan." I finger spelled the name. Because I didn't know how to sign what I wanted to say and the idea of Shawn hitting town was just beginning to strike me as *complicated*, I decided to retreat.

"We were just going to the library," I said, taking Shawn by the hand and giving him a tug so he'd follow me. As we walked, I could feel him looking around.

One of the most interesting things about coming from an aging, insular town is seeing it through the eyes of someone who comes from someplace else. It wasn't the first time I wondered about the potholes in the street or the cracked bricks in the storefront facades, and yet, when I imagined them through Shawn's eyes, its homeliness could have turned a little shabby, its charm a little faded. That's the inevitable consequence of taking something that's precious to you and sharing it with someone else. There's always the fear that it won't measure up.

Yet I knew, as sure as I knew there would be air to breathe as we crossed the street and everyone would be watching us do it, that he would see everything exactly as I saw it. Shawn would overlook the aging and the flaws and find in River Falls the same kind of troubled beauty I did.

"Cool town," he said as we entered the library. I found Mary Lynn in the stacks, and I hate to admit it, but I felt a surge of pride when she did a double take on seeing Shawn. Faint color bloomed in her cheeks and she got a sweet, kind of silly look in her eyes.

"Mary Lynn," I said. "I'd like you to meet Shawn."

Mary Lynn held her hand out and Shawn shook it warmly. "Pleased to meet you," he said in his uninflected voice. Her eyes met mine. I'm dead sure that the look on my face gave away everything I was thinking.

"Shawn is my friend from California. The one I'm trying to learn sign language for."

Mary Lynn's eyebrows rose, and she signed what I could tell were different things about River Falls. I guess she asked him how long he was planning to stay.

"I don't know," Shawn said aloud and signed. "I don't know how long it will take."

"What?" I signed. At least I'd learned something while I was here.

Shawn gave me a sweet smile for my trouble. "I'm just here to collect something that belongs to me," he both signed

and spoke. "And then I hope to be going back to California."
Mary Lynn's fingers strayed to her heart.

Shawn turned to me and spoke. "I'm staying at the
Comfort Inn at the end of Main Street. That's where I'll be,
unless I'm out exploring things around town." He tapped the
pocket of my shirt where I put his spare cell phone. "Keep in
touch," he said, and turned on his heel and left. Mary Lynn
chased after him for a minute, and they exchanged a few
brief signs. I wasn't privy, apparently, to that part of the
conversation because no one spoke. After a minute, she came
back and stood beside me, watching out the window as he
passed by.

"Oh, my." She sighed.

I said nothing but I probably sighed too.

"What was that all about?" I asked.

"I told him to be sure and stop by Hallowed Grounds,"
she said. "That the owner was your sister and she could
probably find him a job."

"This is a train wreck waiting to happen, Mary Lynn," I
told her.

She looked at me very seriously. "What this could be,
Cooper Wyatt, is a way for you to put your past behind you
once and for all and move on. I find I like the prospect of
that very much."

I wondered for a while if I had anything even to say to
that, but when I finally realized I didn't it was too late
anyway. Mary Lynn had moved on.

* * *

"What?" Jordan demanded, and I heard the agitation in his voice. We'd planned a quiet dinner on the patio because the evening air was perfect and balmy, scented with wood smoke from barbecues, and the sun was behind clouds. It was humid with the promise of a good rain before morning.

"I didn't ask him to come here. I never told him where I was. He found me because Jefferson called the references on my job application." I had exchanged texts with Shawn since he'd arrived in town, but I hadn't seen him since then. Stan had apparently wasted no time telling Jordan I had a friend he didn't know.

Jordie sat down on his patio chair hard, placing the plate he'd brought with him in the middle of his place mat carefully, as though if he got it wrong it would matter. "Where's he going to stay?"

"He's staying at the Comfort Inn until he finds someplace else."

Jordie took a bite of his pasta. "But we're supposed to be us. Together." For some reason I noticed how he held his fork. It was quirky, childlike, and had survived both our mothers' efforts to correct it. He picked up his knife and used it to fold linguine onto his fork and with his infantile shovel grip put another bite into his mouth. I loved him. I'd always loved him. But I would never again be *in* love with him.

"I think you need to know that I don't feel the same way about starting over in River Falls that you do, Jordie."

"What do you mean?" He stopped his fork midtwirl.

"I guess I just don't see things the way you do. Being part of the church, being back in our hometown doesn't do the same thing for me that it does for you. I like the library—"

"Coop." Jordie's fork hit the table. "This is about us, dude, the gruesome twosome. It's about getting back what we had."

"What did we have?" I asked him. "What did we have that we were smart enough or sober enough to appreciate when we had it?"

"You've got to call Stan." Jordan got up and started through the slider. "You've got to tell him that you need to talk to him." He disappeared into the apartment.

"Why do I need to talk to *Stan*?" I asked, when he brought me the cordless phone and sat back down.

"You need to tell him how you're feeling. You need to tell him you doubt yourself. You have to let him help you."

"Jordan."

"No, I mean it! Stan can help you. If you have doubts, he can make you see what you need to do to get back the spirit."

"I don't know if I ever *had* the spirit, Jordie, and I don't think talking to Stan's going to help me. I'm fine."

"No, you're not," Jordan said, folding his arms across his chest. "You're not fine."

"What?" I took a sip of cold lemonade and then a deep breath. "What do you mean I'm not fine?"

"You haven't connected with anyone at church. You don't go to meetings. You've blown Stan off when he's tried to help you. Now you're getting back with this guy from someplace you landed when you were rolling around on your motorcycle, running away from who you really are."

I'm sure he was getting ready to go on, but I interrupted him by putting a hand out. "Wait. What?"

"Stan told me. He said you've been running away from who you are and what you've done. He told me he could help you."

"I don't want his help! I don't *need* his help. What if I'm not running away from who I am? What if I'm running toward who I want to become?"

Jordan glared at me. "Because you can do it all by yourself, is that it?"

"Something like that. I can do lots of things by myself, and frankly, I don't even know what it is we're talking about doing!" I calmed my thoughts. "Look. There's no question Stan is there for you, and that's a good thing. I just think for me—"

"Every day," Jordie said. "I wake up in the morning thinking, why the fuck can't I have a damned drink?"

"*What?*" I asked. *Where had that come from?*

"Every day, it's just as hard as the day before. Everything here reminds me. If I'm not thinking about scouts, Little League, raiding the sacrament wine, or rolling around between the pews copping my first feel of your ass, I'm remembering the times when we were little high school fucking *gods*, Coop, thumbing our noses at the small-town assholes and drinking and smoking dope and fucking till we couldn't take a breath anymore!"

Did he see that as the *good* times? No wonder there was no way I could connect with him. "Jordie," I said. "We can't go back to that."

"I know that!" He raked a hand through his hair. "'Cause now I'm remembering the look on Mrs. Johnson's face when she saw Bobby under the wheels of our truck. *Our truck.* Stan tells me that we'll be forgiven. He says that we have a chance to be clean again. It's the only thing that keeps me from taking that drink, trying to score some dope… It's the only thing holding me in place, 'cause not even gravity feels like it's working anymore." He lifted his lemonade to his lips with a shaking hand.

"I get that," I said, hooking a hand around his neck. I squeezed and rubbed little circles on his shoulders to soothe him. "I do."

"So keep coming with me; we can do this. We can find a place where it doesn't follow us. We can do that if we do it *together.*"

"I can't do that, babe." I sighed. "It's not right for me. I don't think it's the same for me as it is for you. I won't drink again. Not because something is keeping me from it, but because it just isn't where I get what I *need* anymore. And I know Stan and the church are giving you what you need; I'm so fucking happy for you, Jordie, you have no idea." I wrapped both arms around him and held him hard. "But I need something different. Something I'm not going to find here in River Falls. Something I don't want to do without anymore."

Jordie pulled away a few inches and looked at me with such contempt. I guess I hadn't seen that before, but it might have been there all along. "I can't decide which is worse," Jordie said, shoving me aside. "That you're an amazing fucking snob, or that you're the world's biggest hypocrite." Jordie left the chair, the patio, and the apartment without a backward glance.

* * *

By eleven that night I had an ashtray full of smoked cigarettes. I called around and no one had seen Jordie, and I assumed the worst. I hoped he'd run to Stan, but I worried that he couldn't handle things and had started drinking again, and that he'd have to go back to day one, back to where it all starts. I was so fucking sorry for him I couldn't even see him as a person anymore. That night I got, for the first time maybe, how deeply fucked my decision to come home and try to help Jordan had been. He was like a drowning man clinging to a lead anchor for safety.

I heard the key in the door, scraping, and waited patiently until Jordan came into the bedroom. I sat in bed, wearing brand-new flannel drawstring pants and an old T-shirt, the ashtray next to me. I had a book, some mystery that my sister had given me, and I'd been reading the first paragraph since about eight, over and over again. He wasn't reeling or walking awkwardly, except maybe he walked slowly, like he was stiff.

"Hey," he said, standing in the doorway, backlit by the light from the hall.

"Hey, Jordie. I was getting worried. You okay?" I had to go carefully. His eyes said something, his body said something, but for once I couldn't read it at all.

"I'm fine." He began to remove his jacket and winced a little.

"Need help?" I asked.

"No. I'm a little…" he murmured, and staggered a bit, and I admit, I guessed he'd been drinking or maybe taking drugs.

I got up quickly and came around him to help him with his coat. "Rough day."

"Thanks." He walked past me to the bathroom, unbuttoning his shirt. As soon as I saw his shoulder revealed in the glow of one of those plug-in nightlights, I had to fight the urge to say something. His skin was covered with marks. I watched him, feeling my blood drain from my face. "You have no idea."

"I guess I don't." I stood there, stunned.

He began to pull down his trousers and I saw thin red slashes, welts, and bruises. Stripes covered his back and down his buttocks, and I guessed from the way he took off his undershorts, down his thighs as well. I watched without understanding at all.

"Jordie?" I stared at his ruined skin. "What the fuck?"

"I needed it," he said simply.

I sat down hard on my side of the bed.

"I need it sometimes. I found out it helps. It's not like you don't know that."

"Jordie, how can it help you?" My past was fueled by alcohol and stupidity. Any kinky pain play, anytime I'd taken that road had been for the rush, the chance to experience just how far I could take my body to the edge. How much further I could push it, allow it to be pushed, before I slid into the darkness and surrendered to it. This was not the same. This was another drug for Jordie, another bite at the apple that he considered safe because it didn't involve street drugs or alcohol. But I knew better. He was playing with the most powerful drugs of all, and he'd allowed himself to get hurt to get high.

He shook his head. "I don't know. I lose myself."

"*Jordie.*" I barely breathed.

"Night, Coop," he said, crawling to his side of the bed. He rolled away from me, presenting the gruesome tableau that was his flesh, and stared at the wall.

"Jordie," I said. I wanted to put my hand on him but I was afraid.

The following day Jordan was gone before I woke up. He'd left a note saying he was going to a meeting before work.

Chapter Fourteen

I probably didn't give Jordan enough credit for trying to work his way back from the past, even though I continued to try to support his efforts. It was never far from my mind that it was my past, too, that we were trying to live down. That night when he got home I asked him if he wanted to go to the grocery store with me. I saw a flash of something in his eyes that I didn't understand, fear maybe, or resignation, but he agreed to go. He was still wearing his uniform shirt from the UPS Store and looked more tired than I'd seen him in a while.

"I'll buy you ice cream," I said without thinking, just like I would have when we were kids. For a minute that seemed to help.

"I can get my own ice cream, Cooper," he said, petulantly.

We walked through the humid early evening together; it wouldn't be dark until nine or so.

"What are you going to make for dinner?" he asked. That was probably more than he'd said in the whole time, and I took it.

"What do you feel like eating?" Fortunately, food was the one thing I could count on to make Jordie talk. He liked all kinds of things, and when he was in the market, he could be easily distracted and talk whether he meant to or not.

"You feel like making some trout?" he asked. "On the grill?"

"Sure," I said. "Let's take a look. Sometimes it's been sitting in the case since the floodwaters of Genesis receded." I felt happy just to be walking with him. There was no denying he would always be my best friend or that I loved him as much today as I always had. Love is a complex thing.

Jordie and I entered the air-conditioned store, and I almost groaned aloud at the pleasure of that cool air hitting my skin. It smelled exactly as it always had, a little meaty, a little like disinfectant, but now that it rented space to a chain java joint, it had the added aroma of good coffee. We got the few nonperishables we needed first, an ingrained habit with me. When you're used to walking to the store, you know what to get last and exactly how long a pint of ice cream has before it melts.

I sent Jordie to choose the ice cream, and I went to get the fish. I found a whole trout that didn't look or smell like my grandfather had caught it before he died, and I was coming down the ice cream aisle when I saw Jordie coming toward me empty-handed.

"What kind of ice cream do you want?" I asked.

"Never mind," he said lightly, but I could see he was holding his body rigid.

"Well, I want some," I told him, and I went down to the frozen case where they kept the pints. "How about Chubby Hubby?" I stopped for a minute to get some frozen hash browns. When I turned back to Jordie, he was standing in front of the ice cream, but there were two men standing in front of the case with their arms folded.

"What the hell?" I muttered and went to ask what was going on. "Jordie?"

He was actually politely waiting for them to move, and they weren't. "Excuse us," I said, thinking it would bring matters to a head.

"No excuse for you," one of them mumbled.

"What?"

"Just move on, Wyatt," the other said. The men had on jeans and T-shirts, standard farmwork clothes around here. They didn't have on the typical trucker hats. They seemed to be just plain guys, although one looked familiar, as if I'd maybe gone to school with one of his siblings or met him when he was young. Chances were we'd known each other, but I didn't think it was recent. They both had dark hair, but one had light gray eyes and one had brown. They looked as hot, dirty, and tired as I felt.

"What's gotten up your ass?" I asked. Usually when you ask a direct question with a big chip on your shoulder, you get an answer or a fist. I wasn't looking for a fist from this guy; he didn't look the type.

"We're the local chapter of *this whole fucking town against drunk drivers*," he said.

"So then I guess you know that neither of us drink," I countered. We were starting to draw a crowd.

"Tell that to Bobby Johnson," the one with light eyes said. "He was my girlfriend's little brother. You remember, don't you? You crashed her graduation party? Came in and drank like you owned the place and killed him on your way out?"

I could feel the tension building under Jordie's skin even though I wasn't touching him. I was sick myself with shock and shame, and I wondered how Jordie could stand there without running or screaming or something.

"I just need my ice cream," I told the man with a shaky voice.

"Then you'll have to go through me to get it," the one who said he was the Johnson girl's boyfriend told us.

"Don't bother, Coop," said Jordie. "You go on ahead, I'll handle this." His voice was low and dangerous and took on a reckless edge he hadn't even had when we were kids and thought we could do no wrong.

"*No*, Jordie."

"Coop." Jordie stayed where he was. "I'll *handle* this."

I looked up at him. I could see it in his eyes, the way they lit up at the thought of a fight. It wasn't like we could for sure beat these guys, and there was no telling how many others in the supermarket were going to come over and help them, but I figured it would be more than would help us. And Jordie would go back to jail.

"It's ice cream, Jordie." I took him by the arm and tried to pull him along. "Not worth it. We're leaving."

"I don't think so." Jordie stayed put.

"Jordan." Pastor Stan was standing behind us. He spoke Jordie's name as if he were saying something important from the pulpit, and Jordie jerked his arm out of mine and turned toward him like a guilty kid. He kept his eyes on the ground.

"Yes, sir?"

Pastor Stan advanced, and the men who'd confronted us looked a little uncertain. Whatever anyone said about Stan's church-of-the-strip-mall, these two were boys who'd been brought up to respect a man of the cloth.

"This isn't our way of solving problems, is it?" Stan asked in his silky voice.

"No, sir," Jordan said.

Stan turned to me. "Would it be all right with you if Jordan came with me for a while?" he asked. I really couldn't say why, but I didn't like the idea, and yet I knew that if Jordie went to a meeting or had someone he trusted to talk to maybe the anger he was feeling would dissipate a little.

"It's fine with me if it's okay with Jordan," I said. I still felt hesitant.

"It's fine," Jordan said. "I think it'd be a good idea."

"Fine then," said Stan, putting an arm out to usher Jordan toward the exit.

"Looks like your boyfriend's stepping out on you," one of the men behind me said.

I turned around and dropped my basket. "You wanna take his place?" The two men stepped away lively enough. Cowards. Jordan, who was on parole, couldn't afford to get into an altercation like this, and they knew it. That was way too close for comfort. Had it gone any further, I'd have knocked Jordan out myself and dragged him home. I found myself leaning my forehead against the cool glass of the freezer case.

A hand touched my shoulder. Expecting a fight, I spun around. Bill Leviton, a local police officer and a guy I had gone to school with, was standing behind me. He had braced himself for trouble, but we both relaxed immediately.

"Is something the matter?" he asked. I thought he recognized me, but he looked *happy* to see me, and I wondered why.

I shook my head.

He gave me a firm handshake. "I haven't seen you since high school."

"Yeah," I said. "Hi." I looked around behind me, but the two men who'd given Jordie such trouble were long gone.

"I got a call there might be a problem here, Cooper." Bill regarded me. *Cop stare.* "Anything you want to talk about?"

I guess I wondered how much I should tell him. "I think it's sorted," I said. Just for the hell of it I grabbed my damned Chubby Hubby ice cream.

"All right," Bill said. He was handsome in his uniform. He'd ditched the hat, or didn't wear one, and had a full head of brown hair. His face was interesting and expressive; he was slightly taller than me but built like a wrestler. He had those white lines around his eyes I always associated with time spent in the sun, maybe fishing. "There's something else, though."

He walked with me toward the front of the store. "What?" I couldn't help it. I still had alarm bells that went off when cops took an interest in me.

He looked around. "I don't want to talk about it here. You came here on foot, didn't you?" he asked. "Can I drive you back to your place?"

"No," I said, as politely as I could.

"What?"

"I said no. I don't do cop cars." I wasn't ready for everyone in the world to know I didn't do cars at all. It wasn't a secret I walked everywhere in town. So far I believed people mostly thought I walked and rode a motorcycle as a healthy and green alternative lifestyle choice.

"Oh," he said. "Well, I have to work anyway. Will you meet me for coffee?"

Did I want to meet Officer Bill for coffee? If I didn't have a suspicion it had to do with Jordan, which I wanted to talk to him about anyway, we wouldn't be having this conversation. "When?"

He looked at his watch. "Eight, maybe? At Hallowed Grounds? I'll meet you."

"Great." Bill shook my hand again. He grinned at me as I put my basket on the conveyor and then he left through the market's double doors.

I paid for my food and hurried home. Having fought for and won my Chubby Hubby, I wasn't going to let it melt on the street.

* * *

"So," Bill said. We'd exhausted all our small talk. Our health and the weather was over two minutes in; our families gotten out of the way before my sister's tattooed barista even began making our giant lattes. Someone brought us pumpkin brownies, which really shouldn't have tasted good, but did.

"I guess you asked me here to talk about Jordan?" I started. "I want to tell you, Bill, that I always thought once a man did his time and served his sentence, he was free to go."

"Well." Bill looked at me like he didn't know what to say.

"And I know he has to keep his parole, but it's going to be hard to do that if people don't give him some kind of a damn chance. We don't need the people of this town holding a grudge and trying to run him off."

"Who's—"

"I mean he's like this big whipped dog. I'm starting to see how this is taking its toll on him. I'm coming to you, man to man. Is there anything you can do to help him? Because one of these days, he's going to get into a fight and they're going to send him back to prison. I'm hoping only about three-fourths of the people in this town want that and that you're in the fourth that doesn't."

"I don't know what you're talking about," Bill said over a particularly loud outburst from a group of teenaged kids at a table near the door.

"Didn't you bring me here to talk about Jordan?"

"Jordan?" Bill asked. "No." Just then something on his face changed, and I sat back in my chair. Bill went from interested and polite to openmouthed and staring into space in a heartbeat.

I turned and caught a glimpse of my sister, who had just come out from behind the bar with a box of decorative mugs.

"Here, let me help you with that," Bill said. He shot to his feet almost instantly and took the box from her, then held it while she put out a new line of ceramics.

I watched for a minute. I could see she was aloof, and yet still not immune to his charms. If he'd asked me here to get that ball rolling and smooth the way for him, things were pretty smooth already. I had my back to the front doors so I was surprised when a gentle hand wrapped itself around the back of my neck. Expecting to see Jordan when I turned, I was shocked to feel Shawn's mouth come down on mine.

In my sister's coffeehouse. In River Falls, Wisconsin.

Silence fell around us for about ten seconds and then the noise became deafening as people tried to cover their embarrassment with conversation. Shawn, who heard none of this, smiled at me and sat down in the seat Bill had vacated. Bill came back, a question clear on his face. His eyebrows were raised and he looked at his coffee cup.

Shawn stood to his full height and stared down at Bill, who was no longer in uniform. I stood as well, to perform introductions, but Shawn beat me to it.

"You must be Jordan." He held out his hand.

Bill shook his head, starting to say who he was way too fast for Shawn to read his lips. I tapped Shawn's arm and he looked at me. I shook my head.

"Bill," I said, signing the name in letters.

"Hello, Bill," Shawn said, clearly confused.

I made the sign for "sister" and said it aloud, and pointed to Julie, and Bill's blush did the rest. Shawn smiled.

We stared at each other for a short time until Julie took pity on us. "Coop? I'll get you some coffees to go and you can show Shawn around town."

"Uh… Well, Bill invited me here to talk," I said, but behind my sister he was rolling his eyes and shaking his head. *When had I gone back in time?* This was so sixth grade. "You've met Shawn?" I asked her.

She smiled warmly. "Yes. I helped him find a job," she told me.

"Yeah?" I turned to Shawn. "Job? Good," I signed. "Where?"

He smiled back. "At an Italian place called Mama Lina's," he signed and said.

I stared at my sister. *Train wreck.* I took my coffee to go and followed Shawn out into Wisconsin's twilight. Briefly, I wondered if Jordie was still with Stan, or where he might be if he wasn't, but I went with Shawn, taking the lead eventually and guiding him to Veterans Park and the free concert there.

"Do they always do this?" Shawn asked me. He was enjoying the vibrations from a very loud band covering country western-inspired rock songs and watching a group of kids whose parents were blowing bubbles for them to chase.

I thumbed, *In the summer, yes. In the winter, their skin would freeze to the guitar strings.*

After a moment, he received the text and laughed. "Small town," he said in my ear. "Like St. Nacho's. Fun."

I was enjoying the music but I looked over and saw a couple of members of Stan's little flock watching me, and I decided I'd like whatever I was doing with Shawn to be more private. Even if we were just talking, by Sunday morning it was sure to be gossip on someone's lips.

I nudged him with my shoulder and indicated that I wanted him to follow me, and even though he was enjoying himself, he came without comment. I led the way down Main Street, and then onto Vine because I had an idea he might like River Falls's own swinging bridge. Built in 1925 over the south fork of the Kinnickinnic River, it just kind of hung there. It wouldn't be too crowded on a Friday night when the band was playing, and it was near enough to the other of River Falls's green spaces, Glen Park, that we could walk a ways on the nature trails. I stood in the middle of the bridge and looked out over the rocks and the water below. Shawn came up behind me, hemming me in between the railing and his big body. He nuzzled into my neck and I could smell mosquito repellant on his skin. *Smart boy.* I didn't wear it, but the mosquitoes didn't bother me much. He gathered me close and just held me there.

"Are you finding what you were looking for here?" he asked against my skin.

My heart was beating so hard in my chest it felt like it was swelling. I could feel my cheeks burn. I felt his arousal at my back. I shook my head.

"Did you miss me?" he asked. "Even a little?"

I closed my eyes. I'm not really a delayed gratification kind of guy, and holding myself back from taking what I wanted? Not something I ordinarily do. So when I felt

Shawn's lips on the side of my throat and his hands—those big, elegant hands of his—slipping down over my abs and into my jeans, reaching for my cock, my first instinct was to drop my head back and say, "Go, baby."

My breathing was already shallow, and I could feel myself leaking onto his ringed hands as they stroked me and reached down to cup my balls. He leaned over and I twisted back so our mouths could meet in a hungry kiss.

"Wait!" I couldn't step away because I was pressed into the rail, so I pushed him a little. "Wait." I was still panting.

Shawn had withdrawn his hands and when I turned he caught me by the shoulders so he could watch me talk. "What?"

"I don't know," I said. I didn't even know what I was thinking; I just knew that if I didn't make things right with Jordan—

"Is it because of him?" Shawn asked. To be fair, it wasn't angry or an accusation. "Jordan?"

I nodded. I got out my phone and held it up, and he took it from me and put it back into my pocket. "It's all right," he said, then caught me by the hand and led me across the rest of the bridge.

We walked a long way, around the park, and for a while we sat in the little fortlike structure on the children's playground. Few people were still around, so we had it to ourselves. I got out a cigarette and struck a match. By the glow of that small flame I looked at Shawn more closely. The planes of his face were lit in such an extraordinary way that I just had to stare. He was beautiful and I loved him. I almost burned myself, but he leaned in and blew the flame out just in time. He took the matches from me and lit another one for my cigarette with a kind of resigned smile. I don't know why we didn't have to talk, but I knew we didn't.

When he reached for me I went to him. He shifted me onto the fort floor in front of him and just let me rest there, against him, smoking my cigarette. At some point, he was running his hands over mine, lacing our fingers together. I crushed out my smoke and turned in his arms. Right then I felt that I had to get close to him. I rubbed my cheek against his stubbly jaw and straddled his legs until our bodies were locked together like a puzzle.

When we started to kiss it was the most natural thing in the world, unhurried and gentle. I put my lips on his neck and I could feel his pulse beat there; his whole body must have been on fire like mine, except neither of us was acting on it. I could feel that rush of pressure in my face as I became more aroused, and I could almost taste the flush blooming under Shawn's skin. But when I put my hands on his belt buckle to remove it—I guess my plan was to suck him off, to give him pleasure—he stopped me.

"Wait," he said.

I rubbed his cock through his jeans. "Let me," I said, knowing he probably couldn't see me too well. At least he must have felt that I spoke because he cupped my face with his hands and thumbed my lips.

I moved down, and he got the idea because he undid his belt and opened his jeans for me. I reached back and pulled out my wallet, feeling for the condom I always kept there. I tore it open with my teeth and rolled it onto Shawn's cock with as much fanfare as I could. I got a hiss for my efforts.

I helped to shift him so that I could get a better strategic position, because this? Was destined to be the best blowjob I had ever given. I slid my hands around to the small of his back and took him as deep as I could, almost pressing my nose into the thatch of hair that formed a V above his beautiful cock. I reached around and teased his ass crack, and he shivered under me, delighting me with a groan, a noise so completely uncalculated and frightening that I thought I heard birds fly out of the trees. I hummed around his skin, bringing one of my hands back, slipping it between his legs to his tightly puckered hole. It only took a few more bobs and a teasing finger and he filled the latex with a moan, clutching my head, stroking my hair, and framing my face with exquisitely gentle hands.

I helped him right his clothes and we climbed down from the fort together. I tossed the condom into the trash as we left the park, walking back by way of the swinging bridge. We stood there, watching the water rush below us by the light of the moon. He put his arms around me from behind.

I heard footsteps running along the wooden boards that made up the noisy floor of the bridge, and then a shriek, a giggle, and two adolescent voices whispering, "*Oh, shit,*" and then louder, "Sorry," as the footsteps ran away. Lots of smothered laughter and a couple of groans.

Shawn was oblivious, except for the feel of feet on the bridge. I could tell he felt that because he turned his head toward the vibrations. Sound definitely played a different role in his life than it did in mine.

He pulled me tighter against his chest, leaning over to whisper in my ear, "I missed you like nothing I could ever have imagined."

Chapter Fifteen

When I got back that night, Stan and Jordan were there, waiting for me. I could tell Jordan was agitated, and Stan seemed to be doing his best to help him. They had their scriptures open on the coffee table. The remains of a pot of coffee added a burned smell to the air in the apartment.

"Where the hell have you been?" Jordan demanded as I set my keys down. I admit hearing Jordan's voice crack over me like that made me freeze in my tracks.

"I was at Grounds with Bill, and then Shawn showed up so I showed him around," I said.

"I'm glad you were so concerned that I was all right."

"I knew you were with Pastor Stan," I said cautiously. "I thought—"

"Jordan." Stan's voice held a small amount of censure.

"That's right," Jordan said. "We must practice Christian forgiveness."

Jordan was more bitter than I'd ever seen him; he fairly shimmered with anger, and even Stan wasn't getting through.

"Jordan, can I make you something to eat?" I asked.

"Yes, because that's going to make everything all better," he said, going into the bedroom and slamming the door.

I looked at Stan. "Do you need anything?"

"Do you think it was wise going out with another man at this point, Cooper?"

I shrugged. Stan might have Jordan's owner's manual but he was still working on figuring out what it took to manipulate me. "That's not exactly what happened, Stan."

"Well, the timing couldn't have been worse, whatever it was," he said, gathering up his things. "And I think abandoning him at this juncture is probably going to have profoundly difficult repercussions."

"I'm not abandoning him," I said.

"He thinks you are," Stan said. He turned and looked at me. "I know you don't have much use for me or for religion for that matter. But Jordan is different. He could become the greatest triumph the Lord has made through me, a man who is wholly given to the Word. He has such a special nature. He's like a child waiting for the Lord to bless him and lead him. And right now he needs me and he needs you to support him."

"I do support him."

"He needs you to join him. To believe in him. And I should think you'd want to show the people of River Falls that two men can change from antisocial teenage monsters into respectable members of the community. If not for Jordan, do it for the people in this town who think all gay men are sexually deviant and indiscriminate. Do it for the people who don't believe two men can share real and lasting love."

He made a good point, and how I wished I could tell him, *Yes, I'm on board, where do I sign.* "I do love Jordan. I have *always* loved him. But I can't be this for him. My love isn't that kind of love. I don't know if it ever was. I don't know what it was beyond the alcohol and the drugs and the stupidity. It wasn't mature or unselfish or based on anything more than history and proximity. It wasn't based on knowing him and understanding the way he saw the world. I don't have that kind of love for him. What I have will last forever. *Forever, Stan.* Through anything. But it's not that kind of love."

"I see." He leaned against the wall, holding that little bag with his Bible in his hand. I could see he hadn't really considered this possibility. That I understood. That I realized how important it was to Jordan, but I just couldn't do it.

"This is going to send him backward to square one," he said finally.

"No, it won't," I said. "I won't let it."

He turned and left.

* * *

"Jordie," I said, knocking.

"Yeah."

"Can I come in?" I asked. There was no lock on the door; we both knew that.

"Yeah."

I walked into the room and Jordie was sitting in the dark fully clothed with his back against the headboard, smoking. I turned on the small bedside light, and he flinched at the brightness of it.

"Talk to me," I said.

"It's not how it was supposed to be," he told me, blowing out a thin stream of blue smoke.

"No, it's not," I agreed.

He looked over at me, and I could see a glimpse of the old Jordie, my fuck-'em-if-they-can't-take-a-joke playmate from the Birch Street Irregulars. "Remember when we figured out how to get beer past the narcs at football games?"

"Yeah," I said. I wouldn't allow him to wallow in the good old days for too long, but I wanted to know where he was going with this.

"Sometimes I think we got away with way too fucking much."

Yeah, okay. Understatement. "Ya *think*?"

He was shaking his head, and just like that, I knew the anger had left his body. We laughed stupidly for a while. He gave me a cigarette and I joined him on the bed, shoving him over.

"We're going to have to quit this," I said, holding the cigarette. "No one smokes anymore. In Southern California they treat you like you have leprosy."

Jordie contemplated that for a while. "We aren't going to happen, are we?"

"No, Jordie, we aren't," I said. "I swear to you it isn't because I don't love you, or because I don't care what happens. I just—"

"You love someone else," he interrupted me. "I could see it when you walked through the door. You looked different somehow. Do you remember when we were kids and you let me fuck you?"

I grimaced. "Yeah."

"I mean later." He chuckled. "When we finally got it right."

"Oh, yeah." I couldn't help it, my breath caught in my throat.

"When you came in you looked like you did then. After."

"I'm sorry," I said.

He was silent for so long. "So."

"Yeah. I didn't remember what that felt like."

"What does it feel like?" he asked. I thought he sounded more tired than angry.

Even so, I asked him, "You don't really want to hear about this, do you?"

"Actually, I think I do," he told me.

"It's warm, Jordie, and it makes you feel really, really good."

"Yeah?"

"Yeah. Better. Bigger. And you want to do stuff that's... I don't know..."

"Noble," Jordie supplied. "I always wanted to be noble."

"No shit?"

"No shit. Like Robin Hood. Or the guy in the war flick who jumps on the grenade."

"I still love you so much, Jordie."

"I know you do, Coop." He patted my back. "I know you do."

* * *

Even though Stan's dire predictions didn't immediately manifest themselves, I still went to bed uneasy. I slept on the couch for the first time since we'd moved in. Jordan did nothing to stop me. When I woke up the next morning, he was just leaving.

"I'm going to a meeting before work." I heard the door shut quietly behind him.

I had work starting at ten, and I wondered if Shawn would be working then as well. I also wondered what kind of trouble he would get us into if he didn't realize that River Falls was not exactly Santo Ignacio and that Mama Lina's was to Nacho's Bar as the Corleone family saga was to *Queer as Folk.*

Shawn, I texted him. *You know River Falls isn't St. Nacho's, right?*

Yeah, he texted back. *So?*

Well Mama Lina's is about as far as you can get from Nacho's bar, I sent.

Duh, came the reply. *You mean I can't blow you in the men's room?*

Duh, I typed back.

How about in the freezer?

They keep FOOD in there, I sent. I put my phone on the kitchen counter and started to make a protein shake.

My phone vibrated. *See you there.*

I thumbed, *See you*. I did that emoticon thing, with the colon and the dash and the parenthesis. I was still shaking my head after I'd showered and it was time for me to leave.

* * *

I was working the food prep area when I spotted Shawn in his busboy getup, as always, with that rubber tub. He turned on his high-voltage smile when he saw me but other than that, he said nothing. Word got around quickly, though, that he was a friend of mine from California, and I heard some speculation about that. People tried to talk to him and seemed to like him well enough. They went to great lengths to communicate, and by the end of the day he was popular enough to be invited for a beer by some of the other guys, which he declined without much effort, saying he had other plans.

I was playing my violin for an older couple having an anniversary when he left. I saw the question in his eyes, and my cell phone buzzed shortly afterward. After I finished my number I took a look. *Meet me? Grounds?*

OK, I typed. *9:00.*

It was the very end of the twilight hour when I made it to Hallowed Grounds on foot. Unlike the night before, I checked in with Jordan to tell him I'd be late. He said he had other plans and I should have a good time.

I felt like I was between worlds, in a state of suspended animation, like in a science-fiction movie where long-range space travel is undertaken by people in big glass coffins who don't age or change while everything around them goes on, business as usual.

There would be little point in sharing my feelings with either Jordan or Shawn. I couldn't tell Jordan because he would try to reassure me that everything was A-okay, and I couldn't tell Shawn because he wouldn't.

I found Shawn sitting at a little bistro table on the sidewalk, completely oblivious to the poetry reading going on inside and piped into the air via a sound system with speakers right above his head. I grinned at him and when I entered the crowded café to buy a latte, I found my sister at a corner table with Bill. Julie was wearing an expression on her face I'd never seen before. Bill had definitely scored a hit. I wouldn't have been surprised to look at her feet and find mismatched shoes; it was that obvious. As soon as she saw me she came over to say hello, and when I got my coffee, we went together back outside to where Shawn was sitting.

The noise from the speakers was deafening so I indicated that I wanted to move the table, and Shawn picked up his coffee with an inquisitive look on his face. My sister pointed up to the speaker, and he realized what it meant and laughed, picking up the chairs to follow us. When we were someplace I could hear myself think, I got out my cell phone and set it on the table.

"Is that how you talk to him?" my sister asked, pointing to the phone and Shawn to sort of include him in the conversation.

"Yeah." I smiled at Shawn and picked up the phone. "He gave it to me back in St. Nacho's, but I didn't bring it home with me. He gave it back to me when he got here."

Shawn smiled back, and I think I heard my sister sigh. Bill joined us then, bringing his cup and saucer. He and my sister shared a special look and I wondered if he'd ever made it home the night before. I could tell Shawn noticed as well because an eyebrow rose on his very expressive face.

"How does Jordan feel about that?" Julie asked me sotto voce, which made me grin a little. Some habits are hard to break. I'm sure she realized that soft or loud, he wouldn't hear her.

"I can't really tell yet," I said. "Sometimes he's angry. Last night he seemed resigned."

"This really isn't a good place for him to be," said Bill.

Immediately, I felt the need to jump to Jordan's defense. "He's done his time," I snapped. It was pretty predictable and caused my sister to roll her eyes.

Shawn watched all this without comment.

Bill softened. "I didn't mean it that way, Cooper," he said. "I want him to succeed. As angry as everyone was—is—about what happened to Bobby Johnson, punishing Jordan Jensen forever isn't going to bring Bobby back. And if Jordan has a chance at a normal life, where he can live in a productive way, I think he should be allowed to live in peace. People around here, though, aren't going to forgive and forget. I wish he'd gone someplace else." Shawn was watching, so I picked up my phone and texted that we were talking about Jordan. He gave me a resigned smile and I shrugged.

"I do too," I said. "Even though I'm glad to be back here. I'm grateful that I can stop worrying that the whole town would run *me* out if I came back home to visit family and friends."

"You didn't really think that," Julie said, like it wasn't a question.

I shrugged again. "It's not like I would have blamed them."

She shook her head. Someone really animated was reading a goofy poem inside, and lots of people were laughing. Shawn stared off into space and I marveled again at how he could be so very *Shawn* in the face of being isolated in his soundless world. I slid a foot over and bumped his instep. He looked at me and I could see that what he missed in sound he more than made up for by visual observation. His eyes scanned me up and down, and I felt flushed when he was done. It was like being touched.

My sister snorted behind her hand. She was making pretty ferocious eye contact with Bill. From inside Grounds, the sounds of laughter, finger snapping, and clapping drifted to us. I heard a sound behind me and turned to find Jordan standing there. I stood, and so did Shawn, and I performed introductions.

"This is Jordan," I signed by finger spelling the name. "Jordan, Shawn." Both men seemed strained but polite. I went to get Jordan a coffee, and when I returned there was an added chair at the tiny table and four people were sitting there warily, waiting for me to come back. I remembered what I thought when I first learned Shawn had come to River Falls: *train wreck.*

I hit on the idea of showing Jordie how to text message Shawn and they got off to a better start, making small talk using the phones. I eyed my sister.

"You and Bill seem to have hit it off," I murmured, close to her ear.

"Tell me you don't think he's too young," she hissed into mine. "Tell me the whole town's not going to start calling me a cougar."

"What? At most, he's five years younger. My age. You don't look your age anyway, Jules." I grinned. "You're hot."

She sighed. "Okay, free coffee for a year if you say that, what? Once a week?"

"Deal," I told her. "So...how was it?"

She refused to meet my eyes. "I don't know what you're talking about." I looked up and saw a strange expression on Shawn's face. I snatched my phone back, wondering what Jordan had said. Jordan looked unrepentant.

"Jordan—" I started to say.

"I was just leaving." Jordan pushed his chair back abruptly. "I had plans; I just wanted to stop by and say hello. Don't wait up."

As he got up, I felt a shift in the atmosphere. A small group of people had gathered across the street, far enough away that I couldn't really make out who they were clearly, or maybe I didn't know them. They stood there staring at Grounds, not moving.

Jordan got up and started walking away, presumably toward our apartment.

"Jensen!" one of the people in the crowd called out. "I see you've got your little pal with you. Looks like he's moved on."

Jordan froze, and I could see Bill frowning, transforming into Officer Bill as he stood up and started walking toward the crosswalk.

"Maybe you should move on too, Jensen," called a woman's voice. "There's no place here where you're welcome."

To her credit, my sister's chair scraped back and she shouted, "Since he's done his time, and he's trying to get his life back together, he is *welcome* here."

"You should be ashamed," the woman yelled back, just as Bill got there and started talking to them. Jordan was still frozen in place. I got up and went to him, meeting Shawn's confused eyes as I did so. I signaled that I'd call him. He nodded.

"Jordie," I began, but that seemed to have the effect of rebooting him, and without turning, he moved on, quickly breaking into a run. I took off after him, only catching up when we reached the apartment.

I made a mental note to stop smoking.

I followed him in and watched as he yanked his cigarettes and lighter from his pocket and tossed his keys down. I started water for tea. When I got to the living room with two cups he was staring out the patio window. I put the cups down on the coffee table and went to him. He shook off my touch.

"Jordie, don't listen to those assholes."

"I don't, not really." He sighed, then took a drag. When he blew out the smoke I opened the slider and closed the screen.

"What a little *mom* you are," he said. "I don't know why I never noticed it before."

I was silent.

"Of course, you were always that way. Taking care of the fuck-up."

"Jordan—"

"Cleaning up my messes."

I didn't argue with that.

"Never mind that half of the mess was always yours too," he said bitterly. "No one could ever see that."

"I saw it," I said quietly. "I *see* it."

"But it never, *ever* touches you, does it? You just keep on keeping on."

"Of course it touches me. I'm tainted with it, of course I am," I said, but I could tell he was working up to something and wasn't listening, and I felt afraid. "Have you talked to Stan today?"

"No, *baby*, I haven't talked to Stan today," he spat, his anger way out of proportion to my question.

"I just asked if you'd talked to Stan. Shit, Jordan. I know it was bad when those people were yelling at you, but—"

"What about you, *hometown hero?* Are you tired of being the prodigal returned yet?"

"*What?*" I asked.

"While you're fucking signing autographs up and down Main Street, I don't suppose it's come to your attention that people wouldn't piss on me if I were on fire."

"Jordan!" I said, shocked.

"As you've no doubt seen, I can't go to the grocery store without people whispering behind my back or confronting me. I can't rent a movie or buy a donut. If it weren't for Stan, I'd have been fired from my job weeks ago. If it weren't for Stan, I couldn't live in this fucking town at all!"

I had to breathe to control my temper. Jordan was like that, had always been prone to outbursts. One of the things I'd learned a long time before was to let him wind down before I began to speak again. "I'm sorry," I said quietly. I lowered my eyes and prepared myself.

"I walk down the street and it's like…I'm an alien. I grew up here. I know all these people, but they look through me like I'm—" He broke off midsentence. "But you don't care about that, do you?"

"What?" *How unfair.* "Of course I care."

"You have a good thing going here," said Jordan. "New job, new lover, family's back together. You drive around on a motorcycle for three years and you've fucking reinvented yourself. Working at Mama's, volunteering at the library, you'll be scooping the horse shit off the street during the Labor Day parade, and everyone will applaud your bony ass while you do it."

"Why are you so angry at *me*?" Damn, but I was so close to losing control.

"You gave me those keys! It was your entire *fucking* fault, Cooper. You made me drive that car, and I killed someone, and now I'll never be all right again." He dissolved into childish tears and threw himself onto our nasty couch, cursing the day I was born. And yet, looking at him, I felt that same protective tenderness I always had, and the crushing weight of sadness. He'd said it. Shifted the blame completely, and now I knew, *I thought I knew*, why I couldn't begin to make things right between us.

"Come here, Jordie," I said, taking him into my arms. He was so completely distraught he came willingly, allowing me to touch him. I pulled him to me and rocked him like a child, like a two-year-old having a temper tantrum. I held him until he was spent and boneless. He removed his sweaty shirt, tossing it onto the floor; I could see fresh stripe marks on his back, probably from a belt, over the old ones he'd gotten before.

"Jordie?" I asked, rubbing light circles on the skin that wasn't damaged.

"Hm?" He arched under my touch, craving it, like a cat.

"Where are you getting these marks?"

He stiffened and turned his face away. "A club," he said.

"What club? Here in River Falls?"

"In the cities," Jordan said, referring to the Twin Cities, before turning to face me. "Look, it doesn't matter where I get the marks, does it? They help me."

"Help you how, Jordie?" I asked him. "I'm not going to judge you, just tell me, all right? How does hurting yourself...letting others hurt you...help?"

"Sometimes I need the pain, Coop. It takes me out of myself to a place where things are okay for a while. It's like I can pay back, for what I've taken."

"Jordie," I said. "All the pain in the world isn't going to—"

He slapped his hand over my mouth. "Don't say it. Don't you say it!" He gave me a look and then his whole face crumpled, like it was burning...melting before me. "You don't have to like it. It helps me." He began to cry and I put my arms around him again.

"Shh, Jordie," I said.

"Nothing's the way I thought it would be, Cooper," he cried. "Nothing."

"I know," I said, wiping spit and snot off his face with my shirt. "Come on, you're making yourself sick."

His hands reached out, and the way he touched me changed from clutching and needy to rank desperation. He pushed me over onto my face, and I fought him hard. We scrabbled and strained. He grabbed my wrists so hard I knew they'd bruise. He put all his effort into making me submit, and I fought just as hard to get him off me. I won, but he had a new black eye and a split lip for his trouble. I had plenty to show for mine, including what was likely to turn into a whopping bruise on my right cheekbone where he'd backhanded me. He went to the bedroom and slammed the door. Later, in the bathroom, I looked at my face in the mirror. All my adult life I'd come to expect little more than

I'd *almost* just gotten. Yet now...now I found I needed more. Wanted more. *Deserved more.* It didn't make sense to demand it from Jordan, who couldn't give it, and it didn't make sense to stay with him and live without it.

I went to sleep feeling as if something inside me had snapped in the night, broken free, and was causing my equilibrium to shift and sway, like something heavy in the hold of a ship that hasn't been lashed down or secured, and is doing unimaginable damage without the crew being aware of it. That was how I felt that night, and the next morning, Jordan was gone.

Chapter Sixteen

I was skimming stock when Shawn arrived at work. He took one look at me and dragged me into the employee bathroom before closing and locking the door. For someone who was always such an emotionally still person, he radiated angry energy.

"What happened?" he asked. He took my shoulders and pulled me under the light, then gently framed my face with his hands and looked at the bruise on my cheek. It was unmistakable. "Did Jordan do this?"

I nodded, holding my scuffed-up hands in fists to show that I'd given as good as I'd gotten. He wasn't amused. He took my hands and pulled the sleeves above my wrists to look at the bruises there. "*Shit.*" He took out his phone and waited. It was a habit that right then, for some reason, I resented. Like he was waiting for me to explain myself. I know that wasn't his intention, but it irritated me all the same.

I took my phone out of my pocket and went through the motions. *It's not as bad as you think*, I texted.

"Yes. It is. Rational people don't do this." He still held himself quietly, even if he was angry, and his implacable condemnation pissed me off.

You weren't there, I typed and sent.

"I didn't have to be there to know that this"—he turned my face to the mirror—"is wrong."

I felt the fight and the excuses leave me. I must have sort of deflated then, because he looked at me with compassion. "I know." I nodded. I put my phone back into my pocket. I had nothing further to say.

He ran a finger over my ears, nudging at my piercings, and down the tattoo on my neck. "You're like one of those prickly"—he poked my barbell—"little hedgehogs." He put his arms around me.

"*Excuse me?*" I asked into his shoulder, but he didn't hear me or care what I'd said. I wasn't feeling the love. In the past twelve hours I'd been called a mom and a hedgehog. I pushed him away.

He was shaking his head. "I know you're tough, Cooper. But there's more to you than that." He put his index finger on the tip of my nose and then flicked my forehead hard, just like he had when we'd met. "Don't let him hit you again, or I'll be tempted to hit you myself." He said this lightly but I felt the steel inside the words.

"I won't." I shook my head even as I rubbed it.

He put his arms around me again and this time I just let him hold me. "Come home with me."

"I can't."

"You're not ready?"

"No. I'm not." Still shaking my head. *I had to learn sign language.*

"You haven't given up, even after this?" His brow furrowed and he let me see his disappointment. "Even after he hit you?" He started to walk to the door, but I caught him back.

"Please don't give up on me either," I said, knowing he couldn't understand.

"What?"

"Nothing." I shrugged.

He gave me a rough hug, said, "*Prickly*," and left me to stare at myself in the mirror.

* * *

Stan came to Mama's while I was playing for the early dinner crowd. He stood in the waiting area and sent me a message via the hostess that he'd like to speak to me. I went to him, bracing myself. I expected him to go on the offensive on Jordie's behalf after the fight we'd had. I approached him and he led me outside where we could speak privately.

He chose not to comment on the bruise on my face. "Have you seen Jordan?" he asked.

"No," I told him. "Not since last night.

He ran a hand through his hair and leaned back against the aging brick wall on the side of the building next to the case that contained a copy of the menu. "He was supposed to meet me earlier today and he didn't show up. I've been calling his cell. It goes straight to voice mail. I take it you had a fight."

"Yes."

"Did he take off last night?" His brows met in a V over his nose. I knew he was concerned about Jordie, but at the time I felt he was part of the problem.

"I don't know. I think he slept at home and took off in the morning. He must have left after I went to sleep; that was about three in the morning. He had some trouble," I said, and told him briefly about the confrontation at Grounds. "He should never have come back here."

"Why did *you* come back?" Stan asked.

"I came back for Jordie," I said. "Otherwise?" I shrugged. I still had my violin and bow in my hand; their weight felt familiar. I was surprised by how much I wanted to lift them to my shoulder and drown him out whenever he started talking.

"Do you care nothing for him?"

I snapped at him, "You're *kidding*, right? Look." I had him hold my bow while I fished in my pocket for my keys. "Here are the keys to our apartment. Go and check that he's not there sleeping or something." I didn't want to say passed out, but it's what we were both worried about. "Check the answering machine too, if you want. Then go to Hallowed Grounds. Tell my sister Jordie is missing and ask her if she can find out anything from Officer Leviton. We can start by eliminating trouble with the law or an accident. I'm pretty sure she has Bill's cell phone number, or he might be there. I'll be there as soon as I can finish up here."

Stan looked at me with troubled eyes, shook his head, and left. Good thing I wasn't trying to win any friends there. He was convinced that I didn't love Jordie. At least I wasn't using Jordie to build my own personal monument to the

Lord. I reentered Mama's and told Jefferson that I'd have to cut the music short. He was nice about it and let me go.

I walked to Hallowed Grounds deep in thought. I knew what we all feared, what none of us were saying, but tried to have more faith in Jordan than that. I looked at the sky because it smelled like rain. Sure enough, fast moving clouds were building and that yellow kind of darkness hung in the air. If I had to say I'd missed one thing when I lived in California, it was this weather. Big thunderhead clouds that loom like mountains on the horizon, the way light changes and affects the very color of the sky, how a major electrical storm feels before it comes, and how it crackles through a person's hair like ghosts.

When I got to Grounds, my sister and her patrons were bringing the tables in from the sidewalk and closing the big double doors. Wind was starting to whip Julie's hair around, and more than one girl had to hold down the hem of a summer dress.

Shawn was there, and when he saw me his face did that happy thing, his smile the one I liked to think of as mine. He came to me and kissed me, establishing that privilege here in Grounds, it seemed, whether I liked it or not. *I did.* Julie came around the counter and gave me a hug. I looked up to see Stan, who had a grim expression on his face. We sat down at one of the larger tables, and the barista brought us all coffee.

"I called Bill," Julie said. "He told me he'd have to do some checking around, but that he hadn't heard anything about Jordan on the River Falls police radio."

"Well, that's good news anyway," said Stan.

"I think he went to the cities," I said. "He was agitated and he would have gone there."

"Why?" Stan asked.

My phone vibrated. When I looked, the text showed a *?* from Shawn. I finger spelled "Jordan" and "gone" in ASL. To his credit, he looked concerned. I'm not sure in his place what I would have felt.

"Why would Jordan go to the cities?" asked Julie.

I hesitated. I looked at Stan, wondering how much he knew. He looked as in the dark as Julie did. "It's possible that he went to a BDSM club. I don't know the name of it or anything. Bill is probably in touch with people who are more knowledgeable. I know that when Jordan is upset he often goes looking for—"

"Preposterous," Stan said.

"And you would know…because?" I asked.

"He's not frequenting places like that. I would know. He confides in me."

"Are you beating him with a belt?" I asked him. "With whips?"

"Of course not!" Stan leaned back in his chair as if I'd struck him. "Of course not, what nonsense."

"Well, someone is. And he told me that he goes to a club in the cities." Stan had nothing to say to that.

Shawn was sitting back, looking interested. Out of every hundred or so words we said, I'd bet he caught ten, and still he sat there politely. It occurred to me that he was a very patient man. I took out the phone he gave me and looked through my contacts. I highlighted Mary Lynn's number and left her a voice mail, asking if she'd come to Grounds when she got off work. I eyed the outside again through the doors. So far it wasn't raining. I thought maybe she could stop by and fill Shawn in before she went home. In the meantime, I tried to text some of what we were discussing to his phone.

BDSM? he sent me back, after I explained that I thought Bill should call any contacts he had in the cities, too. *Why?*

Jordan finds it helps, sometimes, I typed. That hardly touched the surface of why Jordan might feel some relief when he allowed others to harm him. His misuse of pain play was hard to explain. *With stress.*

Shawn gave me an indecipherable look and shrugged. We all sat there in silence, drinking coffee. Shawn was the only one who seemed comfortable with that. I scooted my chair over and took his hand. He smiled at me.

Julie's phone rang and we jumped, but it wasn't anything to do with Jordan. As the evening wore on, we all began to avoid eye contact with Stan, who was calling Jordan and leaving messages at fifteen-minute intervals. Twice, he took off to check my apartment. I let him. I didn't think Jordan would come home if he wasn't taking our calls, but if it made Stan feel better to check, I didn't mind.

Mary Lynn came into Grounds just ahead of the first fat droplets of rain on the sidewalk.

"Hi," she said, giving me a kiss and then leaning over to do the same to Shawn. She greeted Julie and Stan warmly. "I got your message, what's up?"

"Jordie's gone missing," I said. "We're all here waiting to hear from Bill, who's using his contacts to see if Jordie's been hurt, or...or gotten into trouble. I called you because of

Shawn. He just has to sit there, for the most part, watching us talk. It made me feel…"

"I see," she said, and then signed what I'd just said, I guessed, for Shawn. Shawn looked at me and smiled.

"I can't help you very much," he signed, and said. "Even if you tell me what's going on."

"I know," I said, finding that having Mary Lynn as a translator made talking to Shawn almost too easy. "I just… Thank you for being here." I signed "thank you," at least. Shawn put his hand on my shoulder and squeezed.

Bill came in with a bright yellow slicker covering his uniform. "Okay," he said, hanging the coat up on a hook by the door and shaking water off his wet hair. He got a squeal from a couple of high school girls he caught with the droplets.

"Sorry." He grinned sheepishly. "So far no one has any information, and it has to be unofficial for two reasons: One, enough time hasn't gone by to file a missing persons report, and two, we don't want to get him in trouble if he isn't making trouble. It's his perfect right to take off for a day if he needs to."

"Yes, but he wouldn't," said Stan. "Not without telling me."

Julie turned to him. "It's apparent to me that you don't know him as well as you think."

"We have only your brother's word that Jordan has any involvement in—"

"Excuse me?" My sister, heaven bless her, jumped to my defense. "And just why would my brother lie?"

"Perhaps he wishes to hide his own violent nature and is blaming Jordan, just as he's allowed Jordan to take the blame for the accident that killed that boy, Bobby Johnson." Four pairs of eyes, not including mine, regarded him with varying degrees of hostility.

"And just what do you mean by that?" My sister fairly sizzled with indignation.

"I mean your brother has a proven track record of causing trouble and leaving others to deal with the repercussions of that. It's one of the reasons I care so much about Jordan, that he was willing to take on suffering that should have rightfully belonged to someone else."

"Are you on *crack*?" snapped Julie. "You're not from around here, but—"

"Julie, this isn't helping to find Jordan," I said.

"But someone has got to tell this…this person that whatever Jordan's been—"

"Julie—" I began.

"Jordan was violent with Cooper, just last night. The evidence of that is very clear," said Shawn, who had been watching as Mary Lynn translated the conversation.

"We only have Cooper's word for that, and frankly, it makes me just that much more concerned for Jordan."

"Bill, would you please say something?" My sister gripped the sleeve of Bill's uniform. "At least about the accident." All eyes turned to Bill.

"Bobby's accident was before I was on the job here," Bill admitted. "But from what I understand from officers who were first on the scene, that day there were at least three witnesses who said they heard Cooper arguing that he was too impaired to drive, and telling Jordan that they should probably take a nap to sleep it off before they left. That was the reason Cooper was never charged."

Julie looked at him with some curiosity.

"I checked, when he came back to town," he told her. "I knew to expect trouble when Jordan got out, and when I heard your brother was coming back, I looked up the case."

"Why would you do that?" Julie asked him.

Bill reddened under his tanned skin. "Because I wanted to know if I'd need to keep an eye on your little brother." He leaned over to kiss her cheek. "To keep him out of trouble. For you." *Julie's turn to blush.*

"So what you're saying, if I understand correctly, is—" Stan fumbled for words. "Jordan may have...prevaricated about his role in Bobby Johnson's accident?"

Mary Lynn, who was still signing the whole conversation for Shawn, spoke. "At the time it was quite clear. Jordan and Cooper had words and Cooper urged Jordan to stay at the party. Cooper said he was unable to drive. Jordan argued that he was fine and asked for their truck keys. Cooper handed them over and they left, and on the way out of the driveway, Jordan struck and killed Bobby Johnson, who was riding a tricycle on the sidewalk behind them and couldn't be seen in the rearview mirror as the truck pulled out."

Mary Lynn said this so matter-of-factly that I hardly even realized she was talking about me. When she got to the word tricycle, though, I had the sensation of being sucker punched and experienced a kind of electric shock of shame. I couldn't look at anyone at that table. Like a coward, I put my head down on my arms. I had cried every tear I was capable of crying over Bobby Johnson in rehab. Now I was just numb. I felt a strong hand on my back and looked up to find Shawn's eyes on me. They were filled with compassion and love. Right then, his faith in me was unbearable.

Outside, the rain was beginning to come down in torrents, and the wind was whipping it so that it didn't fall straight to the earth. I remembered what Jordan had said about feeling like not even gravity worked anymore, and found I *did* have more tears for Bobby Johnson, after all, and plenty more where they came from for Jordan, as well.

Chapter Seventeen

Ten o'clock is closing time at Hallowed Grounds on Sundays. When it rolled around, we were all still sitting there, drinking coffee and worrying about Jordan. Someone had gone to the deli and gotten an assortment of submarine sandwiches and chips, which my sister cut into fourths and served buffet-style. There were only a handful of other patrons because the weather became fiercer by the minute.

Great slashes of lightning lit the sky and thunder rattled the windows. Shawn looked concerned. I put a hand on his arm to get his attention. "Mary Lynn, would you reassure Shawn that this isn't the apocalypse? I think the weather is making him nervous."

Mary Lynn signed something and Shawn shook his head, looking a little embarrassed. "We don't have weather like this in Santo Ignacio. I can feel the thunder." He put his hand on his chest.

I laced my fingers with his other hand and kissed him lightly on the cheek. "You get used to it," I told him and Mary Lynn signed.

"I hope not," he countered.

"I didn't plan to stay out this late," said Mary Lynn, looking at the clock. "Mark told me he didn't want me to leave until it let up, but I can't stay all night." She got up and moved away a little distance to call her husband on her cell phone.

I took the opportunity to use a few signs on Shawn—asking if he was all right and offering him something more to drink. He seemed delighted that I tried. My sister got up to begin closing everything down, and the rest of us, Stan included, helped her out.

"I really should be going," Mary Lynn said.

I could see she was hesitating. "It's all right," I told her. "You've helped out so much. Thanks."

"I hope everything's all right with Jordan. Would you call me the minute you find out where he is? Even if it's the middle of the night?"

"I will," I said. "I promise. Is your car here or at the library?"

"Here." She rolled her eyes. "I felt like such an idiot driving it two blocks, but now I'm glad I did." I took my sister's umbrella and held it over her head as I walked her out to the diagonal spot her car occupied at the curb and she got inside. As usual, the umbrella helped not at all, and I was soaked to my skin when I returned to the coffee shop.

My sister gave me a minuscule towel to dry myself off. Shawn, who was wearing a short-sleeved shirt over a long-sleeved T, gave me his outer shirt. I pulled mine off over my head to put his on and my sister stared hard at my back.

Stan, who had said very little for most of the evening, spoke. "I see you, too, are a practitioner of the entertainments you claim Jordan is seeking." He gestured toward my back with its thin scars.

"I got those scars from someone who would never be considered even remotely connected to any legitimate part of the BDSM community. That was revenge." I'd never talked about it, but it wasn't a secret. "Someone was angry with me for something bad I did. I'm not proud of it. I scar easily." I took out my cell phone, sorry Mary Lynn was no longer with us, and filled Shawn in. *Talking about my scars*, I sent.

He nodded.

Later, I typed. There was no point. To Stan, I said while I tried to type just enough to keep Shawn in the loop, "For Jordan, finding the place where pain turns into numbness is going to feel like a drug. When he gets very anxious, he always looks for a way to escape. That's my theory about why he may do it. He's found that pain takes him outside himself for a short time. I guess he needs that sometimes."

Stan compressed his lips into a thin, disapproving line.

Shawn texted me, *Do you need that?*

No. I don't, I typed. *I don't find I run away much anymore.*

"Good," Shawn said. He took my hand and kissed the knuckles. I smiled. Stan made an impatient sound.

"Why isn't he calling?" He ran a hand through his thinning hair. His boyish face looked old. Whatever else there was to say about Stan, he did care about Jordan, and he was taking this very hard.

"Jordan is complicated," I reminded him. "He isn't like other people. He's angry and hurt and disappointed and scared. And he feels guilty still. He's never really been able to face that."

"I had hoped I'd helped," Stan muttered. He looked like he was about to make this more about him than Jordan. Something about that made me angrier than was strictly necessary, so I got up and walked to the window.

The storm raged outside and water was beginning to seep under the doors. I got some towels and laid them over the puddles.

"I've got to do something," Julie said behind me. "I'm going to go to my office and start calling hospitals in the city."

Bill stood up. "I'll go with you." They went together, hand in hand, leaving me alone with Shawn and Stan.

I met Shawn's eyes and couldn't help rolling mine.

"I think I'll go check your apartment again, just in case," Stan said, getting up and heading for the door. I rolled away the towels and let him out, and then I closed the door and leaned my head against the glass. In no time, I felt Shawn's arms wrap around me.

"Why don't you play for me?" he asked. "While we wait." My violin was tucked behind the bar where I'd stashed it when I'd gotten here from work. "It will take your mind off it."

I sat in one of my sister's comfortable overstuffed couches with my feet up and noodled around. I could put the instrument to my shoulder with Shawn resting his head beside it, and he would feel the music as if he were playing it. We sat that way while I played Mendelssohn's "Violin Concerto in E Minor" until Stan came back.

He sat quietly in a chair on the other side of the room. When I stopped, Stan said, "You're very gifted."

"Thank you." I started to put away the instrument.

"Don't stop on my account. I find it rather...soothing," he admitted.

I continued, playing whatever pieces came to mind. Sometimes it was hard to hear the music over the storm. After a while, Julie came out and sat down with Stan. I felt Shawn drifting off to sleep, his body relaxing and his breathing evening out. His large hand with its many rings drifted to my lap in a perfectly innocent way. Right onto my dick. It made me smile, but I didn't stop playing.

There was a loud noise from the office, and Bill rushed in. "I've found him," he said. "He's all right. At least I think he is."

I stopped playing so abruptly that the motion woke Shawn. I finger spelled "Jordan" and "found." Then I moved my hands up and down like I was balancing something to indicate "maybe." I said a silent thank-you to Mary Lynn for teaching me that sign.

"He was in a private BDSM club as a guest of one of the members," Bill said, and I took out my phone.

Shawn covered it with his hand and said, "Later." I nodded.

"He was unruly," Bill was saying. "He didn't want to leave when they asked him to. They felt he'd had enough, and he got argumentative."

I cringed. I hoped to hell he hadn't done anything that would get him sent back to prison.

"They put him out," Bill continued. "And called the police."

My heart sank. "Is he in jail?"

"No," Bill said. "He's at United Hospital. He's all right. He asked to be taken there."

"What?" I asked. I was trying to make sense of everything Bill was telling me, but it wasn't clear. I was tired and I'd had an emotional day. I felt my violin begin to slip from my fingers and jumped, only to realize that Shawn was trying to take it from me to help put it away. I smiled at him and he leaned over to kiss my cheek.

"According to the officer who took the call," Bill said, "Jordan said he felt like he should go to the hospital. He asked for a voluntary commitment."

I shook my head. I didn't understand. "I want to see him."

"I'll take you," said Bill, already getting his coat. "You might need me. It's a piss-poor night to drive. I'll bring my truck around." He unlocked the doors and went out into the rain, which was lashing down. I was numb or I would have realized what he'd said. An enormous black Silverado crew cab pulled up lit like an emergency vehicle. I stared at it in shock. Stan was already headed out the door to meet him, and my sister was waiting for Shawn and me to exit so she could go last and lock up. I was frozen in place; the realization that they were all waiting hadn't yet broken over me. I eyed that black truck, and the worst day of my life replayed itself over and over in my head like a song I couldn't get rid of.

I took a big step backward, nearly knocking Julie over in the process. Stan and Bill were staring at me from inside the vehicle. Only Shawn understood what was happening.

"Can we have a minute?" he asked my sister, who looked at me like I was a stranger.

"I have to lock up." She waved her keys.

Shawn took them from her and said, "Go, I'll lock up. I want to talk to Cooper."

Julie left through the door and skittered out into the rain, leaping into the truck and closing the door behind her to keep the rain out. Lightning illuminated Shawn's face.

"Do you want to go?" he asked me simply.

I nodded.

"But you're afraid."

I nodded again.

He flicked my forehead, then kissed me like a soldier on V-J Day. "Better get over it, then. You need to be there for Jordan, and you're not going to be able go by bike on a night like this. You have to remember what's important."

Leave it to someone who had never heard me speak to understand me so clearly.

I started to panic and then to argue, but he pushed me out the door into the rain. He turned to lock the door behind him, and I had to run to the truck because I still had my instrument, and even in its case, my instinct to preserve it was more powerful than my fear. But only until I got into the truck. Once there, I found myself seated next to Stan as

Shawn leaped in on the other side of me, and I started to have the mother of all panic attacks.

"Drive," Shawn told Bill, who had turned to me when I got in. Bill raised his eyebrows but said nothing, turning back around, pulling out onto the empty street, and heading for the highway into the cities.

"What's wrong?" Julie asked me. I kept my eyes closed. I was shaking and beads of sweat were popping out on my skin. It was completely hopeless to explain. Stan watched me as though I were a science experiment, but Shawn understood and tried to help. He crushed me to him and whispered nonsense into my ear.

"You're doing fine," he said. "Breathe, baby."

I put my head down on his shoulder and he never stopped talking. At first I had to gasp for breath to control the nausea I was feeling, but then all I could smell was Shawn's skin, still moist from the rain, the warmth and richness of his essence currently scented with Italian food and coffee and my cigarettes. I sank into that, inhaled it, let it surround and engulf me. His lips next to my ear, teasing the skin there, and the words he said, all conspired to make me feel, if not comfortable, capable of the forty-five minute drive to the hospital in the cities.

By the time we got there, I was so anxious I could have had myself committed. I was covered in sweat and I'm sure I stank. I took it as a victory that I wasn't covered in puke. I stumbled stupidly over Shawn to climb out of the truck and fell into a puddle of rain on the pavement below on the way out. I might have been crying.

Julie and Shawn picked me up while Stan and Bill stood a small distance away, trying not to look.

Shawn said something in Julie's ear and she looked at me like I had grown two heads. No one said anything else, though, and we stumbled together through the rain into the hospital's emergency entrance. It was an indication of my state of mind that I left my instrument in the truck because normally I would never just leave it in a car.

* * *

Past history and hard mileage have made me wary of the police. I've never been proud of the way my eyes hit the floor when there are cops around, but I've never been able to change it. But having Bill there in uniform gave us the kind of credibility we needed to get information and I made a vow to give any preconceived notions I had when seeing a cop in uniform a significant overhaul. Bill spoke quietly but respectfully to the emergency room admitting clerks and told them we were there for Jordan Jensen. He asked for and secured permission to see him, and when he returned it was with the news that Jordan would see me, and only me, privately.

Stan was crushed, and he covered it poorly with pastoral concern. He tried to tell me what to say and how to say it and begged me to ask Jordan to allow him in, but I'd have been less than honest if I agreed. As I walked down the sterile corridor, I worried that I might have been too hard on Stan, but overall I felt admitting visitors was up to Jordan, and I wasn't about to try to sell Stan as an answer to his problems.

I entered the small room. It was a rehab room; it contained a small bed, a nightstand, a little table, and a chair. It didn't have the medical equipment of a traditional hospital room, nor did it yet have the reassuring personal touches of a lengthy habitation. Just seeing it made me crave a cigarette and a cup of coffee.

Jordan was lying on his small bed, facing the wall. I knew he could tell when I entered. I wasn't stealthy. He didn't react, though, and I decided to sit in the small office-type chair and gather my thoughts.

"Did you ride your motorcycle in this fucking miserable storm?" he finally spoke.

"I came in Bill's truck with Stan, Shawn, and Julie. We're all here. Mary Lynn was concerned. I told Bill to call her."

He turned over and stared at me, hard. "You rode in Bill's truck?"

"How else was I going to get here without getting myself killed?"

His eyes shimmered. He turned back over and lay down facing the wall. "You must think I'm an asshole," he said.

I rubbed my face. Sometimes I stalled if I didn't know what to say.

"It doesn't matter what I do, Bobby is still *always* there."

"He is," I agreed.

"It's not the same for you," he snapped.

I didn't point out that he'd made it the same. That he'd wanted me to own the responsibility for Bobby's death entirely. "You can't know that."

"I do know that," he said in the smallest voice. "Even though I tried to make everyone think—" He sighed. "I *do* know that."

I got up and went to stand by the side of his bed, looking down at him. He looked small, somehow, and I knew I would never see him as a grown man. He'd always be Jordie, the boy I loved. The brother I wanted. The lover I'd lost in alcohol and confusion and tragedy. I lay down behind him and pulled him into my arms, fitting our bodies together carefully because he hissed in pain. I told him everything I ever knew about him and me and us. I begged him to hear me, finally, and understand.

It was dawn when he finally fell asleep.

Chapter Eighteen

The first thing I did was leave the building for a cigarette. This severely pissed off Stan, who had been waiting all night to see Jordan.

"He doesn't want to see anyone," I told him. I could see he didn't believe me but I was tired and didn't give a fuck.

"He saw you," Stan pointed out.

How tired do you have to be to feel like kicking a member of the clergy? "Well, yeah, Stan. Because I'm not just *anyone*," I said, turning away.

Shawn came out the double doors and picked his way through the crackling tension to stand beside me. "How is he?" Shawn asked, taking out his phone. He put his free hand on my shoulder and gripped it a little, I thought, to let me know I should rein it in.

"Angry," I said, for Stan's benefit, as I typed for Shawn's, *Remorseful, guilty, depressed.*

Shawn leaned over and put his lips on the side of my neck and nuzzled in with a sigh, pulling me to him. "Sorry," he whispered.

I took a deep drag of my cigarette, hoping it would help stop the shaking in my hands. *More later*, I typed with one thumb. He read it over my shoulder, so I didn't bother sending.

Bill came out of the hospital to join us, pulling my sister along behind him. She had marks on her face where she'd slept on him; his uniform button had impressed itself on her cheek below her right eye. She still looked tired.

"Jordan wants us to go home," I told them, encapsulating hours of conversation. "He doesn't want to see anyone. He wants to go to Hazelden and try rehab again. He says he wasn't honest the first time, when he was in prison. He won't be coming back to River Falls."

I felt Pastor Stan stiffen beside me. Since he'd taken Jordie's success so personally, it only followed that he'd take this the same way.

"I'm sure if I could talk to him—" He started back toward the hospital doors.

Bill caught his arm. "If he doesn't want to see you, you can't—"

"He'll see me; I know he'll see me. What are you?" he asked me, turning and raking me with a nasty look. "Just his old *drinking pal.* Of course he'll see me; I offer him the water of life from the Savior himself." He might have been self-righteous. He also might have been right, but so long as Jordie remained dishonest inside of himself, it wouldn't matter. If he was going to tell himself the truth, finally, I was all for it. And I didn't think he could do that with us around. Jordie had asked me to leave; it was hard but it was right. And I loved him enough to do it.

Looking at Stan, though, I felt sorry for him. I was searching for something to tell him that might make him feel better when my sister said, "Oh, for the love of heaven, put a *sock* in it," and walked past him toward the truck.

I don't think I had ever loved her more.

* * *

Bill dropped Shawn and me off in front of the apartment I shared with Jordan. It wasn't easy, but I didn't claw my way out of the truck. The panic attacks seemed to be able to bypass my brain and travel directly to my nervous system, so that when we exited the vehicle, I was still wet with sweat and drawing shaky breaths. I acknowledged my sister, Bill, and Stan, and took Shawn's hand to go inside.

I felt all wrong. As soon as I entered, I knew it was only a matter of a few days before I would leave the apartment entirely. I was actually hoping that I wouldn't have to spend another night under this roof. Shawn bumped into my back when I stopped moving forward.

"What?" he asked.

I got out my phone to text him. I couldn't wait until I could learn enough sign language to avoid needing this interface between us. *I can't stay here.*

? he texted back.

I don't belong here, I texted. *I never did.*

Shawn smiled a little. "Get what you need and come with me."

I shook my head. *I have to clean.* He moved so he could read over my shoulder. *I have to pack. Take stuff to his mom. I have to give notice and*

His hand closed over mine and his mouth came down on my lips. "Not today, you don't," he said.

I acknowledged that he might be right when his hand strayed to my ass. I grabbed my helmet and Jordie's for Shawn, and we headed for the Comfort Inn on my bike.

What started in the empty elevator continued down the deserted hallway until we reached Shawn's room. The little red light on the door lock no sooner turned green than he was pulling on the handle and we were spilling through, rubbing and groping each other until we almost fell over. He pushed my back against the door and it became clear why hotels bolted that "for your safety" government-mandated evacuation plan there rather than just hanging it on a hook. He was shoving against me hard, and I was completely okay with it, desperate to get to a little patch of his skin to lick or suck or bite.

I wrapped my legs around his waist when he slid his hands under to cup my butt. He dug his fingers in, teasing the crack of my ass, and when I shoved hard against him in response he staggered with me to the bed. We flopped there inelegantly, but it felt so good to fucking feel him hard against my body again that I grunted and fought for some kind of dominance. He wouldn't let me have it, though, and he slipped his hands inside my jeans and grabbed my naked skin.

We rolled and stretched and twisted, and I brought my knee up against his balls to give him some quality friction when I saw the lube and condoms on his nightstand. I extended a hand as far as it would go to grab for them. As luck would have it, at that exact moment he rolled me over, pushing my legs apart to hump against me, and I slipped off the slick chintz bedspread, headed for the floor with my head.

"Fuck!" I threw a hand out as I went down, knocking the lamp off the table amid a spray of sparks and broken light bulb glass. When Shawn tried to catch me, he slid along on top of me, grinding me down into the hard hotel floor under his body.

Shawn grabbed me quickly and rolled with me, until I was on top of him and we were both panting, our hearts slamming in our chests.

Shawn lay beneath me, blinking. Finally, he sighed. "That went well."

* * *

We tried a more leisurely approach until the ice stopped the bleeding from my scalp. I straddled Shawn's lap while he held the ice in place and we just…kissed. I don't know if I had a concussion and that's what made it seem dreamlike, but the warmth and solid perfection of being there, finally, with Shawn, planning to go home to California together— without the need for words—stole my breath. Some television show was playing music, and I hummed the tune into his skin. He rocked me back and forth as we surrendered to our senses. He started to undress himself then, and I pulled my shirt, or rather his shirt, over my head. We put the ice in the sink and shucked off the rest of our clothes and by tacit agreement met back at the bed.

I knew I didn't want to lie down. My head hurt, and I was afraid friction would make it bleed again. On the other hand I was flushed and aroused and there was nothing in the world I wanted more than for Shawn to fuck me. He sat back on the bed and got the condoms and lube. We avoided the broken glass on the floor as I climbed up on the bed. When I would have straddled him, he pushed me to all fours. He smoothed his hands over my ass and began to kiss and lick me, slipping that slick, talented tongue down my spine and into my crack, teasing at my hole. He thumbed my ass cheeks apart and blew a thin stream of air, giving me that delicious frisson of cool on wet skin, and when he pointed his tongue and pushed inside I thought I'd die.

"Oh, Shawn," I moaned. I dropped my head forward, which hurt like *fuck*. "Shawn, don't wanna—"

Shawn's finger replaced his mouth, and he massaged my ass open, grabbing the lube with the other hand and deliberately dropping a dollop of cold goo on me while he fucked me with his hand. He shoved a second finger in, catching the lube with it, and his fingers started to glide and curve around until he had me bucking against him like a kid.

I reached back to drag him toward me and heard him tear a condom packet with his teeth.

"Oh, *yes.*" I turned my head and reached for his dick. He slapped my hand away with a grin, then rolled the condom down and pulled me back, teasing at my ass with his cock. I pushed myself back as he moved forward, holding me steady, watching himself sink into me. He groaned and pulled me up, my back to his chest, and he filled and stretched me until I thought I'd tear apart. I gripped the top of the headboard and held on. His hands explored my torso, then cupped my cock and balls.

I let him set the pace. At times he surged into me and jerked hard, and at times he moved languidly, slow and deep. It seemed like he was less interested in where we were going than how we got there.

I knew I would follow him back to California and live whatever life he wanted us to live. I knew I would stay with him for as long as he let me. I knew that I would learn to speak his language and love his friends; that I could add richness and meaning to his life, as well as my own, if I just grabbed him with both hands and clung.

"Love you," he ground out as I shuddered to a climax around him. He pulled me to him so tightly that I almost cried out. He pumped my cock lazily; I was still riding on a crest of sensation as he jerked to his own orgasm and filled the latex inside my body. He pushed his forehead into the meaty part of my shoulder and pressed hard, still jerking inside me. "Love you, love you, love you," he murmured against my skin. I put my hand back to capture his head, wanting to hold him too, just as tightly.

* * *

In the end, everything I owned still fit into four file boxes. I sent the boxes to Nacho's Bar from the same UPS Store where Jordie had worked. I saw Shawn off from Minneapolis/St. Paul Airport the following weekend. He chose to fly instead of riding on the back of my motorcycle and even though he gave me all kinds of shit about not going on a road trip with him in a car, I still loved him.

I saw Jordie settled at Hazelden. He was subdued. He felt stupid because he wasn't using, and who the hell goes to rehab clean? Still, he told me privately that he was always only two breaths away from a total meltdown and that he thought he'd like to see if he could stretch that out. I admired him for his courage. He probably wouldn't have believed me, so I didn't tell him.

At any rate, I didn't get the chance because he had me thrown out. He was smiling when he did it, but it didn't make it any easier. He said he had to start thinking in terms that didn't include me. I said *good fucking luck with that*, and that Shawn and I would be coming to see him, probably at Christmas.

"Oh, yeah," Jordie said tiredly around a thin stream of cigarette smoke. "'Cause Christmas in Minnesota is every couple's dream vacation. Stay and build your life there," he told me. "I'll stop by and visit when I'm ready."

I hugged him to me hard, and he held me just as hard right back.

"You give me hope, Coop," he told me, as he walked away from me.

"For you?" I asked. "I have all the hope in the world." I wanted to stay. I wanted to be there and let him lean on me. I wanted to give him my strength, such as it was, and my last drop of blood if that's what it took. He did that little squeezy-fisted wave thing that people do when they want to piss you off and then he left me standing outside.

Oh, fuck, I kept repeating in my head until I got to my bike. Everything I needed for the next few days was there, just a small duffel and my violin, strapped on it. It was ready to go and so was I.

But it hurt.

I said "I'll be back" more than Arnold Schwarzenegger before I hit I-90, the interstate that cuts across the northern plains states. I knew I'd never feel right until I could see Jordan would be okay. We were connected like that. As the days passed, though, and I rode across the country through the endless miles of whispering grasses under the wide-open sky, I began to look forward to getting home. And nowhere would ever be home to me again but St. Nacho's.

I took the interstate all the way to Seattle, and then came down the I-5 and then California State Route 1, Pacific Coast Highway. I made remarkable time. I knew that no way would Shawn be expecting me when I arrived, dirty and tired, and parked my bike in the Nacho's parking lot. The air was crisp with a briny tang and blew at my matted hair when I took off my helmet. A thousand smells emanated from the bar, but the ones I'd missed most, that mixture of cumin and onions and the oily smell of chips frying, hit my nose like Christmas morning.

"Well, hot holy fucking hell," said Jim, coming to the end of the bar to give me a bear hug. "How the hell are you?"

"Fine," I said, even as he tried to sever my spine.

"I've got to call Alfred; he and I had a private wager, and I just won it. Well"—he hesitated—"are you planning to stay?"

"Yes. If I can. Can I stay upstairs again, or do you have a new hard-luck case you're working on?"

Jim rolled his eyes. "The only hard case I see"—he flicked my instrument—"is this one. Welcome back, son."

"Glad to be back." I couldn't help myself. My eyes traveled to the edges of the bar in search of Shawn.

"He's not here right now, but he'll be back soon," Jim told me. "I sent him to get some things at the office supply store. You have time to shower, if you're quick."

I didn't hesitate. I went out and grabbed my duffel before coming back in and running up the stairs. I showered fast and shaved faster, and then put on clothes and went in search of Shawn. On the way I was stopped by a number of people, and I stopped in to see Oscar and Tomas, whose good-natured teasing turned exuberant when they found out I was home to stay.

"Hey, m'hijo," said Oscar, giving me an affectionate hug. "It hasn't been the same, man."

Tomas jumped me from behind, teasing. "Yeah, bro, where'd you put the knives? We've been buying our veg precut. Too bad you don't got a job around here no more."

"That's not how you say it," Oscar chided. "Don't you know English? It's *too bad you don't got a job around here no more, asshole.*"

"When you are right, you are right, papi. What a difference a word makes. So much more *muy espléndido.*"

Oscar followed me out onto the beach when I went out to smoke. "Good to have you back, m'hijo," he told me, all teasing put aside for a moment while we stood with our cigarettes on the boardwalk. "You know they're trying to ban smoking here on the beach, and the boardwalk? Lung-police fuckers."

"It's time we quit anyway, Oscar. We're not getting younger," I said. I didn't like the idea of quitting, but I liked the idea of exposing Shawn to my secondhand smoke even less.

Oscar sighed. "I suppose so," he said. "I just hate to do what I'm told."

"I'm figuring on quitting before someone tells me to," I said. "Should I get you some of those nicotine patches too?" I'll admit I was teasing, but it seemed like he might be liking the idea. What the fuck? I crumpled up my pack and tossed it in the garbage. "More money for me, man. Think of how much we'll save. After we're done with the patches anyway. What are you going to spend it on?"

Oscar didn't hesitate. "Condoms and lube. Tomas wants me to quit so bad he's made all kinds of promises. I think I'll let him think it's his idea for a while."

I laughed. "Good thinking," I said. Out of the corner of my eye I saw Shawn's white Toyota Camry pull up, the one that belonged to his sister but that he sometimes drove. He got out and began pulling boxes out of the trunk. I could tell the exact moment when he realized that my motorcycle was parked in the parking lot. It wasn't very difficult. He dropped everything onto the pavement and came running straight at me. He didn't stop until he'd picked me up and flung me around a little, and I had to hide my face in his shoulder because everyone was staring at me for all the wrong reasons.

I wrapped my arms and legs around him and let him drag me inside and up the stairs. In the background I could hear laughter and good-natured ribbing. I heard Jim complaining about having to pick his office supplies up off the pavement in the parking lot, and threatening to call Alfred over to explain the importance of yellow pads and Post-It flags.

"St. Nacho's, man," I heard Oscar say. "What're you gonna do? Everybody who sets foot in this town changes."

"Yeah," said Tomas. "But the smart ones like you, papi, they just keep on changing the same."

"I got news for you, pendejo; I quit smoking. Prepare to be my newest crutch."

I snorted.

Shawn closed the door and locked it. We stayed that way, locked together in a coming-home hug, for a while.

He pulled back just enough so he could see my lips. "Are you glad you came back?"

I sighed and licked a path up his neck. He tasted hot and salty and delicious. I took a deep breath and then met his wonderful golden brown eyes. I took my hands off his shoulders, prepared, at last, to put into practice all the things I'd learned from the books Mary Lynn had given me. I began to sign, starting with, "I'm glad to be home," but he grabbed my hands and picked me up and dropped me on the bed.

He paused above me for the barest minute to smile warmly down at me. "You talk too much."

THE END

Z. A. Maxfield

Z. A. Maxfield is a fifth generation native of Los Angeles, although she now lives in the O.C. She started writing in 2006 on a dare from her children and never looked back. Pathologically disorganized, and perennially optimistic, she writes as much as she can, reads as much as she dares, and enjoys her time with family and friends. If anyone asks her how a wife and mother of four manages to find time for a writing career, she'll answer, "It's amazing what you can do if you completely give up housework."

Check out her website at http://www.zamaxfield.com.

TITLES AVAILABLE In Print from Loose Id®

ALTERED HEART
Kate Steele

CROSSING BORDERS
Z. A. Maxfield

DANGEROUS CRAVINGS
Evangeline Anderson

DARK ELVES: TAKEN
Jet Mykles

DARK ELVES: SALVATION
Jet Mykles

DARK ELVES: DISCOVERY
Jet Mykles

FAITH & FIDELITY
Tere Michaels

FORGOTTEN SONG
Ally Blue

HAWKEYE ONE: DANGER ZONE

Sierra Cartwright

HEAVEN SENT: HELL & PURGATORY

Jet Mykles

HEAVEN SENT 2

Jet Mykles

INTERSTELLAR SERVICE & DISCIPLINE:
VICTORIOUS STAR

Morgan Hawke

RUSH IN THE DARK: COMMON POWERS 2

Lynn Lorenz

SHARDS OF THE MIND:
THE TA'E'SHA CHRONICLES, BOOK TWO

Theolyn Boese

SLAVE BOY

Evangeline Anderson

SOMETHING MORE

Amanda Young

SOUL BONDS: COMMON POWERS 1
Lynn Lorenz

THE ASSIGNMENT
Evangeline Anderson

THE BITE BEFORE CHRISTMAS
Laura Baumbach, Sedonia Guillone, and Kit Tunstall

THE BROKEN H
J. L. Langley

THE RIVALS: SETTLER'S MINE 1
Mechele Armstrong

THE TIN STAR
J. L. Langley

Publisher's Note: The print titles listed above were previously released in e-book format by Loose Id®.

CPSIA information can be obtained at www.ICGtesting.com
Printed in the USA
LVOW091655300911

248619LV00001B/16/P